SLEEPER

BRUCE CROWTHER

WALKER AND COMPANY
New York

The Sleeper stood at the window of the first floor bedroom and watched the high April clouds race across the sky intermittently obscuring then revealing the moon. He half turned as his wife moved and sighed on the bed behind him. He looked across at her and smiled gently for an instant then his face sobered and he turned back to look out over the quiet garden. As always when he looked out of that particular window he found it hard to accept that he was in the heart of London, the place was so secluded and sheltered from sounds and unwanted visitors.

*　　*　　*

The waiting had not worried him for a long time. Years in fact since he had last felt the stirring of unrest and impatience that troubled him now. After he had first been placed in England he had accepted that he would not be activated for some years. That, after all, was the object of the exercise and he had enjoyed the first five years as he had established himself and familiarised himself with his new home and the background taken from the dead soldier he had replaced. Then he had begun to wonder if he had been forgotten and as the years passed he was frequently tempted to use the emergency contact. He never did and on the tenth anniversary of his placing he had heard. The message had been terse and explicit, one word: wait. He had waited and over the following years as he had risen in his chosen field he had not expected to be called. It was obvious that the longer he was left the higher he would rise and the more useful he would become to his masters. Nevertheless he half expected to hear

5

on the twentieth anniversary and he had not been disappointed. That time the message had been a little more human, it was also twice as long, two words: congratulations, wait.

*　　*　　*

In the past ten years he had continued to gain in authority and power and again he did not expect to be called. Even so as the thirtieth anniversary approached he began to worry. He was fifty-four years of age. More than half his life had been spent in alien England and for reasons he knew lay deep in his subconscious he began to think more and more about his almost forgotten homeland.

He wondered whether he had created a problem for his masters by his astonishing success. He had risen so fast and so high he doubted there was much they could use him for. Certainly none of the routine tasks Sleepers were used for would come his way. He would not be wasted on anything other than a project of maximum importance and they seldom came along. He thought about lighting another cigarette and then decided against it. He had been smoking far too much recently. He would cut down. He walked over to the bed and slipped in beside his wife. She turned towards him in her sleep and embraced him. He lay on his back and stared at the ceiling for a long time waiting for sleep to come.

*　　*　　*

The Sleeper might have slept more easily had he known that at the same moment thousands of miles away he was uppermost in the thoughts of three men, his masters. The conference had been in progress for several hours and the room was littered with papers and the air was acrid with the smoke from many cigars and cigarettes. Empty glasses and cups and the remains of several meals bore testimony to a long hard session. The three men were relaxing for a moment and as always it was the old man who spoke first. His

6

voice was a pained scraping gasp that made his listeners wonder if his sentences would complete.

" Then we are agreed."

" Yes." The first to answer was a stocky aggressive sounding and mannered man who reached and implemented decisions rapidly and who had obviously chafed at the protracted discussion that had just ended. The third man was, as always, slow to speak. He resembled the old man in many ways and although the youngest of the three, there were few who doubted that when the old man died he would replace him. As if to underline his position as heir apparent he always made his comments last, putting the decisions of the group into words and with his own decision carrying to the chosen course of action a not inconsiderable weight.

" The choice of action at our disposal is limited. Severely limited. That part I do not like but we have to accept it. What is important is that we do it exactly as we discussed. There must be no deviation and therefore we have to be sure that everyone who participates is the best man for his particular part in the proceedings."

" Of course," the other young man spoke with some asperity, " I would have thought that was a matter of course."

" None of this will be a matter of course. This has to be faultless."

" It will be." The old man cut in and ended the bickering. " Is there any doubt about any of the personnel in London?"

" No, the Sleeper there is the best man we have. His achievements testify to that."

" Still, thirty years is a long time," the stocky man interjected, " should we check him first?"

" No, too risky. He is special. We can rely on him. What about his contact. Who is he now?" The stocky man pushed a file across the table and the others studied it carefully.

" Not as good as he could have been but his involvement

7

will be minimal."

"What about afterwards?"

"The usual action will be taken." There was a silence as all three thought of the same thing together. The old man was the first to speak again.

"I take it we are agreed on Stellman?"

"Yes."

"Yes. If he will do it. He won't need the money."

"He will do it. It is precisely the kind of deal he likes."

"How much will you offer?"

"The same as last time."

"He won't like that, it was years ago, even assassins are victims of inflation." The old man looked bleak at the less than serious tone in the stocky man's voice.

"This is easier."

"Still it has been a long time," the third man put in quietly.

"Very well. Plus twenty percent."

"Plus fifty would be better."

"A million and a half. Nonsense. Alright then, plus thirty. No more." The old man leaned back in his chair and closed his eyes to signify the end of the meeting. The other two rose and murmured their farewells and left the room. Outside they stopped and conversed for a moment.

"Will you make contact with Stellman?" the stocky man asked.

"Yes. You notify the contact and send a message to the Sleeper. It is the thirtieth anniversary in a few days. Then will be soon enough."

"Thirty years. We were still school children. Perhaps we should have him checked again."

"No. The old man said not. And I would be a little more careful with him if I were you. He dislikes levity and for that matter so do I." He turned away quickly before the stocky man's face could colour and embarrass them both.

ONE

Stellman stepped onto the tarmac at Gatwick Airport and followed the courier and his fellow passengers up the canopied steps that led to the long corridor. He swung his hand luggage lightly as he walked with the others. It was his first visit to England and he was looking forward to it. With the object of his visit far back in his mind he felt almost like a tourist.

*   *   *

Two weeks before, in the middle of June, a man looking remarkably like Stellman had boarded a package holiday flight bound for Faro in Portugal. The holiday had been booked with a firm of travel agents in London that specialised in villa holidays and who were suffering like a lot of other agents from falling bookings. They had been happy to stretch their resources to make the last-minute booking especially when the man had said he wanted the holiday so much he was prepared to take a three-person villa for himself.

Once in Portugal the man had spent his two weeks at the villa and then after leaving his carefully wrapped passport and driving licence with the bartender at the Hotel Eva in Faro, he had headed for the interior with a rucksack and pup-tent. Stellman took his place on the return flight. The other passengers had not seen the other man since the out-

9

ward flight and they had not noticed the slight facial difference. In another two weeks time Stellman would leave England on another package holiday booked by the same man but with a different agent and a different tour company and two weeks after that the first man would return. The cycle would be complete and Stellman would be back in Portugal. Then with his own passport he would disappear again and the other man would return to England and would never know, although he might well guess, why he had spent six weeks in the sun at considerable expense to others.

*　　*　　*

Stellman handed the passport to the Immigration official and looked at the man with no trace of nerves which was not surprising for it was too early for him to be feeling the tension that would build later. The official glanced at the passport and handed it back. Stellman waited with the other passengers until their baggage came clattering out of the escalator and onto the revolving deck. He picked out his single case and headed for the green-lit walkway. A few minutes later he was in the main hallway and he grinned slightly to himself at the ease with which he had entered the country. It would be nice, he thought, nice but unlikely if the rest of his visit went as smoothly.

*　　*　　*

He decided that a cup of coffee and some food would be a good way to start as he had several hours travelling before he would be able to stop moving. He walked up the stairs to the upper floor and joined the queue in one of the restaurants. The food was dull and stodgy but he had travelled enough to defer judgement of British cooking until he was

10

in somewhere less rushed. By the time he had eaten, his coffee was cold and he pushed it to one side and headed for the main hall once more. He made no attempt to look out for watchers. He was not known, he was not expected, he was not worried and in any event attempting to look for watchers in the milling mob of holiday-makers and other travellers was impossible. Not that he intended taking chances. Before he stopped that night he would have covered and recovered his tracks.

*   *   *

He followed the signs through to the railway platform and bought a ticket for Victoria. The frequency of the service was such that he was waiting for only a few minutes before he was able to board the train. He was pleased the flight had landed in daylight and what he saw of the countryside matched his previously formed opinions about the scenery. He leaned back against the prickly upholstery and turned his attention briefly to the others in the compartment. They looked precisely what they were. Ordinary people returning from their single annual holiday to take up where they had left off in the unequal struggle to survive. He felt nothing for them. Once he would have felt contempt, but then he had been young. Later he would have felt pity but the years had rubbed from him any true concern for his fellows. Now he felt nothing. They did not exist.

*   *   *

If they looked at him at all the others in the compartment certainly spared him no thoughts. The slightly-built insignificant man in the corner. A trained eye might have noticed that the tan was deeper than the result of two weeks sunshine a year and a very well trained and astute eye would

11

have observed that the quietness was not that of insignificance but the repose of a man having total confidence in himself.

*　　*　　*

The train pulled into Victoria less than an hour after it had left Gatwick and Stellman walked out of the station concourse and looked around him savouring for a moment his first, admittedly uninspiring, sight of London. He followed his mental plan of the streets around the station and without hesitation he reached the Hertz office. He gave the name on the passport and the young lady checked the booking form.

"Oh yes, here we are Mr. Carter, a Hillman Avenger." It took only a few minutes for Stellman to complete the formalities. He had practised the indecipherable scrawl Carter called a signature and the similarity between his effort and the signature on Carter's driving licence was enough to pass the casual glance given by the young lady.

*　　*　　*

He joined the late afternoon traffic and he had no time to worry that he had not driven in a city's traffic for many years as he was swept along with the rush, his instincts taking over and getting him safely through to the suburbs. He had headed generally southwards from Victoria following no particular path as he drove along unfamiliar streets. By six o'clock he was in Streatham and he pulled into a side road and took a street map from his suitcase.

He located his position without difficulty and he plotted a fairly direct route to his destination. Half way along he traced his finger on a circular detour that would serve the purpose he needed. He folded the map carefully to expose the area he was in and restarted the car. For the first time he began to watch his rear-view mirror. The new caution was not totally unnecessary. His employers knew he was in England and so did his contact in London and so too did the man at that moment hiking through the hills of Portugal. He was not worried about his employers, his previous involvement with them had shown them to be as reliable if as ruthless as he was himself. He was not really worried about Carter for he knew nothing of the man who had taken his passport.

His contact was a different matter. He was a young man. Although Stellman had never met him he had obtained a comprehensive dossier from his employers. Still only forty-five or so, he was never absolutely sure of his date of birth, Stellman preferred to work with older men. Not that he found them any more reliable, they were simply more predictable and that gave him a feeling of control. The contact knew Stellman was special but he did not know how special and he certainly did not know why Stellman was in England. Stellman knew that that lack of knowledge might well be the spur to curiosity and that was the most dangerous thing of all. Up to collecting the car from Hertz the contact knew Stellman's movements. Now all that remained was for Stellman to change cars so there would be no possibility for the contact to use the Hillman's registration number to track him.

*   *   *

He drove steadily and carefully until he reached his detour point. He drove round in a wide circle watching all cars on the road in front and behind him until he was doubly sure that he was unwatched. He rejoined his route and picked up a little speed.

*　　*　　*

He reached Gatwick at about eight o'clock and the light was starting to fade. He parked the Hillman in one of the many privately owned car parks adjoining the airport. He booked it in for four weeks and gave the real Carter's return flight number as he completed the form. That took care of the Hillman and he waited in the mini-bus for the car park driver to take him and a few others the short distance down the road to the airport. Once there he quickly rented another car, this time a Godfrey Davis Ford Cortina and within half an hour he left Gatwick for the second time that day.

*　　*　　*

He headed west through narrow tree-hung lanes with no real knowledge of where he was, content to know that so long as he drove towards the still light sky he would eventually reach the main London to Portsmouth road. When he did he stopped briefly to check his location then he re-started, turning south on to the main road. He reached the motel after only a few minutes driving and turning in he parked the Cortina outside the reception area.

*　　*　　*

He completed the registration form in the name of a man he had once known. The receptionist was obviously near the end of her spell of duty. She was tired and hardly looked at Stellman. A neatly printed sign over the desk told him he still had time to get a meal in the motel's dining room. He went out to the Cortina and took his suitcase and hand luggage into the small motel room. He washed and shaved

14

and put on a clean shirt before going into the dining room.

* * *

He knew his room had been burgled within seconds of opening the door. He could not identify what it was that told him. There was no outward sign. It could have been a faint residual smell left by the intruder or it might have been the simple animal instinct that had kept him alive and unharmed for many years. Whatever it was he did not argue with it. He had not unpacked. The shirt he had taken off lay where he had left it and his shaving gear was on the surround of the room corner wash basin. Everything else was in the suitcase or the briefcase. He went through them quickly. There was only the smallest signs of disturbance.

Nothing had been taken as only clothes were there. His wallet, the passport and other papers never left his person. He sat on the bed. He never considered for a moment that he was the only subject of the intruder, he was completely confident that he was clear of all surveillance. It had to be the work of a sneak thief and that meant the police would be around. Stellman had two courses of action open to him. One was to go quickly and risk being a suspect of the police. The second was to stay and be interviewed along with the rest of the victims he was certain there would be. The decision was easy. He had several days left before he had to begin work. Ample time to disappear and reappear elsewhere and his description when the police asked for it would be necessarily vague as apart from the receptionist he had spoken only to the waitress in the dining room. He stood up and quickly repacked his case. He took the hand towel and began a careful and systematic clean-up of the room. When he was through he walked quietly out to his car and drove away into the night.

*   *   *

Raymond Adams was tired. Not just tired after a long and very hard night's work but tired in a deeper sense. He had always enjoyed being a policeman and now as Commissioner of the Metropolitan Police he had reached the very top after what had been a near-meteoric rise to power and authority. But he was tired. Somehow the kick, the enthusiasm, had waned. Not suddenly. It had been a slow change in attitude over the past few years and it worried him.

He stretched and yawned and closed the file open before him. He had reached out an arm to turn off the desk light when the telephone rang. For a moment he thought about not answering it but the thought was an indulgence he knew he would not allow himself. He sighed quietly and redirected his hand from the lamp to the telephone.

" Yes?"

" Chief Inspector Andrews is on the line sir. From finger-prints. He did say it was important."

" Put him on." Adams delved into his memory and came up with a hazy mental picture of Andrews. A small fussily precise man with sandy hair and a permanently polluting pipe. The voice matched the picture he had of the man. No particular accent and nothing particularly memorable but precise in its manner.

" Andrews speaking sir. Fingerprints. We have turned up a white code print on the computer. I thought you would like to know at once." Adams sat up straighter. The finger-print files at the Yard had gradually expanded over the years until eventually and inevitably they had installed a massive computer. Any print sent in by any Division or any outside organisation that had been granted the facility was coded

16

and sent through the computer. If the prints were on file the file reference was turned up by the machine. Certain files were designated with colour codes meaning an interested party outside the United Kingdom. Blue meant the man or woman concerned was wanted. A red code was a man or woman who might or might not be wanted but either way was classed as dangerous. The white code was a very different matter. So far as Adams knew there were only two or at the most three white codes in the computer. The matching data files were all sealed and designated Most Secret.

" Send up the file, no, you'd better bring it up yourself."

" Right away sir." Commissioner Adams sat looking at the telephone for a moment. He hoped against hope that the computer might have made an error. The last thing he wanted at the moment was a case involving international complications for he knew the data had been fed in by an outside organisation. It could have been any one of a hundred overseas police forces or any one of a dozen or more secret service organisations, their own and a few friendly states. Andrews brought the sealed file and stood and waited for the Commissioner to open it. There was one small sheet of paper inside and the Commissioner read it at a glance.

" Tell me the background."

" The print came in from Surrey County sir. A motel burglary down near Hindhead. I don't know the details. The officer requesting the check was an Inspector Walters. I ran the data through the prints on file, turned up nothing and then ran it through the unknown marks. That's when it turned up this file."

" Thank you Chief Inspector. Leave it with me will you?"

" Yes sir." After Andrews had left the Commissioner reached for the telephone once more and dialled the number he read off the slip of paper the sealed file had held. After a moment the telephone was answered. Adams told the switchboard operator at the United States Embassy who he

17

was and asked for the name on the slip of paper.

" Colonel Hunt is off duty at the moment sir, can anyone else be of assistance?"

" Can you connect me with Colonel Hunt by any means at all? This is important."

" Hold the line please sir." Adams waited and in what seemed like only seconds he heard a sharp and alert voice.

" Commissioner Adams?"

" Yes, Colonel Hunt? I'm sorry to wake you at this hour."

" That is alright Commissioner, I expect there is a good reason."

" That's for you to say Colonel. You know that you have certain fingerprints recorded in our computer with a request for notification should one turn up?"

" Yes."

" One has turned up."

" Do you have the reference we gave it?" Adams looked down at the slip of paper.

" A number, two seven two." He heard clearly the indrawn hiss of breath from the man at the other end of the telephone and instinctively felt a quickening of his pulse. He did not know who Colonel Hunt was but he would have bet a month's pay he did not usually display his feelings. The silence lengthened.

" Colonel?"

" Sorry Commissioner. I won't pretend you haven't turned up something special. Can I come down there now?"

" Of course. The man in charge of the fingerprint division is Chief Inspector Andrews."

" If it isn't an imposition Commissioner could you be there? If there is no error we will want some very high level co-operation."

" I'll be here."

" Good. There won't be much traffic at this time in the morning. I'll be with you inside half an hour." Adams re-

18

placed the receiver and thought for a moment then he picked it up again and was connected to Andrews in a few seconds.

"Chief Inspector. Run that print through again will you, just to be sure."

"I have done sir, no doubt it's the one."

"Thank you Chief Inspector." Adams replaced the receiver and thought for a moment. He glanced at his watch. If the American was to be on time he had another twenty or more minutes. He decided not to waste them.

* * *

Colonel Hunt was punctual. He was shown into the Commissioner's office within a minute of his estimated arrival time. With him was a slightly-built man, dark haired, dark complexioned and with a hard edgy appearance made softer by owl-like horn-rimmed glasses. Hunt was one of the few Americans Adams knew who could be described as typically American. Tall, straight, slightly gangling with an open but shrewd face, he even had the short hair and rimless glasses that had so often been parodied.

"Commissioner, a pleasure to meet you. This is a colleague of mine Lewis Comoy."

"Colonel, Mr. Comoy. Sit down please. Tea or coffee?"

"Coffee if it can be arranged." Comoy nodded agreement. The Commissioner made the call and then spread his hands on the desk in front of him. He waited.

"The prints you have Commissioner. First question has to be, and I hope you'll forgive me, is there any possibility of an error?"

"We've checked. The print our people sent in is a match for those you have on record in the computer. Naturally we can and will arrange an analysis by one of our best people but for the moment you can assume they are the same." Colonel Hunt leaned forward before he asked his next ques-

19

tion and Adams sensed the tension the two men felt as they waited for his answer.

" The man whose prints you have taken, is he in custody?"

" No Colonel he isn't." The two men sat back and Adams saw the intense disappointment on Comoy's face. The other man gave no outward sign of concern but Adams knew instinctively that he was just as disappointed.

" Commissioner I must presume certain things and I hope you'll forgive me. There is very little I can tell you, at this stage, and I may never be able to give you all the story."

" I understand Colonel, don't let that worry you."

" Can you give us the background?"

" Yes of course, while I was waiting for you I spoke to the officer who sent in the prints for checking. The circumstances are these. There has been a spate of motel robberies over the past week or so. All within a fifty or sixty mile radius of London and all following a similar pattern. Never more than a dozen rooms done and all between dinner-time and midnight when the guests were out of their rooms. Always cash and valuables and no clues as to the identity of the men responsible."

" Men?" Comoy asked the question.

" Yes, we are fairly certain there is more than one man. The number of rooms done in the time available make it almost impossible for one man to have carried out the thefts unaided. We think two though it could be more." Adams paused as a knock at the door preceded a uniformed policewoman carrying a large tray with coffee and biscuits and, Adams noted approvingly, doughnuts. The American Colonel grinned slightly but refrained from comment. After the police officer had left the cups were distributed and the Commissioner took up the story once more.

" Several county forces are involved but liaison is pretty good and there is general agreement on these points. There has been nothing to tie any guest into the robberies. Until

20

last night. The motel in question is down near Hindhead in Surrey, about fifty miles from here. Last night eight rooms appear to have been entered. Naturally when the police were called the officer in charge, an Inspector Walters, made certain enquiries. He checked first to find if any other rooms had been robbed and he found one guest missing. He didn't think anything of it at first, thought the man was out late. When it became obvious to the Inspector that he had another in the sequence of motel robberies on his hands he temporarily lost interest in the missing guest. He put a fingerprint team into the rooms that were reported to have been entered and they came up with what you would expect. A mess.

Guests, staff, dozens of prints and a pretty smeary lot they were too. By the time he had finished questioning the guests and staff Walters realised it was very late and there was still no sign of the missing guest. He had the manager open up the room and Walters went in on his own. It was obvious the man had gone. No clothing or personal articles of any kind. Walters sent in the fingerprint team. They found no prints at all. The room had been wiped clean. That naturally told Walters he was on to something, connected or not with the robberies. He had the room re-checked and they came up blank again. Then he had a bright idea. He checked with the dining room staff. The missing man had dined alone. He'd arrived late and had a cold supper. The table had been cleared of cutlery and so on but the menu card was still there. It was a typed card inserted in a plastic folder, you know the kind of thing. The card had been typed that day and the folders are regularly wiped clean. Walters had it checked.

There were three sets of prints. He eliminated two, the girl who typed the card and the waitress who served the man. The remaining set did not match with any other set taken at the motel. That is the set he sent here for checking by the computer, after he'd drawn blank at his own head-quarters." Adams leaned back and eyed the two Americans speculatively. They were looking at one another and Adams had no doubt that whatever it was Surrey County Constabulary had stumbled upon it was a matter of the very greatest importance to these men. Hunt stood up abruptly and walked over to the window. Quite suddenly without anything being said Adams was aware there had been a subtle shift in the relationship between the two men. Comoy had taken charge and Adams looked at the small man with interest.

"Thank you Commissioner. That was very clear. Your Inspector Walters seems to be an intelligent man. I would like to meet him." The remark was clearly not intended as a casual comment.

"When?"

"As soon as possible. Is he still on duty?"

"Yes he is waiting for me to call him back."

"Good, the Colonel and I would like to drive down there immediately we could be there in, what, an hour?"

"Allow yourself nearer two. The early morning traffic will slow you leaving the city."

"Please telephone the Inspector and tell him we'll be with him in two hours. And would you ask him if he would be kind enough to tell us all he can?"

"Of course. Can I also tell him that this man, whoever he is, is not involved in the robberies?" Comoy grinned slightly with his mouth.

"Yes you can tell him that Commissioner. Undoubtedly our man spotted that his own room had been burgled and decided to get out fast." Comoy stood up and the Colonel turned away from the window. The three men shook hands and the two Americans left Adams alone. For a moment the Commissioner thought about going home to get the night's sleep he had lost then he decided against it and pulled the telephone towards him. He would make peace with his wife

22

and then shave before making a start on another day's problems.

* * *

The two Americans sat silently in the Embassy car as the chauffeur drove swiftly through the thickening traffic. Hunt was the first to break the silence.

" Damn it we didn't make a physical check of the prints."

" There's time for that later. We want to see what other signs there are. And get a description of him."

" My God." Apparently Hunt had not realised the implications of the story Commissioner Adams had told them. " My God. The waitress. She's seen him. And she's talked to him. She can describe him. After all this time we'll know what he looks like."

Comoy said nothing. He stared into the streets flowing past the car and tried not to give way to the burning excitement he felt. All those years of hunting for a shadow. A shadow he had decided over and over again was non-existent. He sank lower into the seat as he felt the excitement suddenly drain out of him. The disappointments of the past had been too many. This would be like all the other leads. It would come to nothing. They always did.

* * *

Stellman had driven through most of the night. Backwards and forwards through narrow English lanes. Up and down short stretches of trunk roads and motorway. The driving had had three purposes. It had effectively blinded any trail he might have left. It had passed away the night less obtrusively than parking would have done. It had also relaxed him a little. He had experienced the first signs of tension as he had cleaned out the room at the motel. It was too early.

23

He did not want to begin the build up for some days yet, he knew the danger of being too tense, too taut, so that an unexpected event could cause him to react too sharply.

Suddenly he felt hungry. He hadn't eaten since supper at the motel. It was still early when he pulled into a roadside cafe. Designed to cater for truckdrivers, it had a plain anonymity that suited him. He sat at a table. He was alone in the room. He reached for the piece of well used and slightly dirty card that served as a menu and he stopped as if he had been turned to stone.

In his mind he saw the white typed card in the plastic folder with the crest of the motel. It had been clean. Spotlessly clean. Probably typed ready for the following day and it would have on it three sets of prints. The typist's, the waitress's and his. Any others? He doubted it. Would the police think of it? He had to assume they would. There was no doubt the waitress, a friendly chattering girl, would remember him and be able to describe him clearly. Would it matter. As far as he knew his fingerprints were not on record anywhere. He could take a chance. He could always take a chance but Stellman knew he would not. He had not survived so long by taking chances.

*   *   *

He went out to the Cortina and studied the map. Directly, without the random turns and twists he had taken through the night he could reach the motel in under an hour. He started the motor and went off fast.

*   *   *

Harry Walters yawned widely and drank the remains of his, what was it? His twentieth cup of coffee. He thanked the small angel of mercy that had sent him to a motel to investigate a crime. It could have been somewhere less comfortable. In fact it usually was. He wondered about the calls he had had from the Yard.

Talking to the Commissioner himself was an event he doubted would be repeated if he lived to be very old. He also wondered who the two Americans were. The Commissioner's second call had told him to give every assistance and he had no doubt that he had stumbled into something big. The robbery he was investigating was nothing to concern the Americans or the Commissioner for that matter. He scratched his chin and grimaced at the bristles he felt. He decided to shave and tidy himself up. Then he would send someone round to wake up the girl. He had questioned her after he had had her prints taken for elimination. Her description of the man had been reasonably good and he felt that the girl would probably be able to build up a good likeness when the Photo-Fit arrived.

But it was obvious the excitement of the evening had been too much for her. That and working for almost as many hours at a stretch as a policeman. He had decided to let her go to the room she shared with one of the other waitresses for a few hours. She would be better for the rest. Another half hour or so and he would feel better as well. Ready to start work on the Photo-Fit picture.

*   *   *

Fifteen miles from the motel the Embassy car was stuck in the middle of a traffic jam on the Guildford by-pass. A heavy and extra wide load had come to an unscheduled stop with a burst tyre and traffic police had not yet arrived to organise things. The chauffeur switched off the engine and lit a cigarette.

Twelve miles from the motel on another road Stellman forced the Cortina along at marginally over the speed limit.

He could not risk being stopped by the police but neither could he risk losing a minute.

*   *   *

In the single bed in the double room she shared at the motel, the object of more attention than she had ever enjoyed in her life was fast asleep dreaming dreams of excitement and adventure.

TWO

The Cabinet meeting had gone badly for the Foreign Secretary and he sat glowering in the Prime Minister's study. He took no part in the conversation between the Prime Minister and the Home Secretary even though the subject did concern him indirectly.

"Michael, you must not let yourself be provoked so easily. You usually ride out the kind of unpleasantness we had today."

Michael Ainsley sat upright and tuned back into the conversation realising that his black mood had penetrated the atmosphere and caused the Prime Minister to break off the conversation he had been having.

"No, I know that Charles," he answered, "perhaps I am letting myself be irritated a little too readily these days. Do I risk losing my job if I say I'm tired and more than usually overworked at the moment?"

"I doubt you will lose your job for that." Charles Fox smiled the easy smile that was worth many thousands of uncommitted votes every time he appeared on television at election time. "If tiredness and overwork were the operative criteria then I think we would all lose our jobs." Fox turned back to the Home Secretary, Peter Evans, and resumed the discussion with Ainsley, suitably if gently chastened, paying close attention. "The security operation is of course the matter of gravest concern particularly as the conference was set up at such short notice. The question that has to be asked is, are we up to it?" Evans scratched his nose thoughtfully and frowned at the desk top.

"Up to it in the sense of knowing what to do and how to do it, yes we are. The main difficulty as always in matters like this is manpower. The police are no less under strength than they were the last time we had a major conference in London."

"Then we are in a worse position because we have never had a conference quite like this one. Not in modern times at least."

Ainsley nodded agreement at the Prime Minister's remark. "I agree," he said, "but are we looking for trouble that isn't going to be there? I accept that to have the President of the United States and the Premiers of Russia and China and France all here at the same time is unusual but so also is the mood of the people of all these countries. For the first time since heaven knows when, there is a fairly high level of accord. There are no wars or police actions, no revolutions."

"True, Michael, but if you will forgive a small touch of cynicism, that is precisely what worries me most. I have the uneasy feeling of the calm before the storm. We must guard against being lulled into carelessness or worse underestimating the seriousness of the potential danger to individuals during their stay here. Peter, what about the security staff of the individual governments? What has been agreed so far?"

"We have given almost unlimited freedom insofar as

numbers are concerned. There is little point in doing otherwise. We have no real way of limiting the security staff attached to any of the embassies and it seemed simpler to let the various countries make whatever arrangements they wanted. We have however, restricted the number of security men who will be in close attendance at the meetings and on the journeys between the embassies and the conference centres. We have also placed a limit on the number of firearms to be carried by these same men."

"Why? I cannot see the difference in terms of a security risk if a member of the French staff carries one revolver or two, or if the total fire power of one Embassy exceeds another. As far as we know they are not going to attack one another."

"A matter of checking. If we know in advance how many men are supposed to be in any one place at any particular time and how many weapons they have between them, then spot checks can be made and made effectively."

"Are you sure the proposed searches and inspections can be carried out without too much friction?"

"As certain as we can be. Each control team will include one national from each country involved. These men have been grouped so that while they probably cannot all speak each other's language, there will be enough multi-linguists to cover the problems of failing communications."

"What about our own auxiliary security force. They've been in operation for how long? Three years? Any problems there?"

"No, they have proved better than we expected. And they have certainly reduced pressure on the police and the special services departments."

"Good. Well we can no doubt rest reasonably easy that all points are covered." Charles Fox leaned back in his chair and looked across at the Foreign Secretary.

"Are the agenda agreed for the opening meetings?"

"Yes. No difficulties there if you discount the obligatory French niggling."

"Dear me. What was that you said about accord?"

"Well you know the French. Never agree if you can possibly disagree and discomfit the other side."

"Even when the other side are supposedly on the same side eh?"

"Precisely."

"Very well then, that seems to be all we can do for the present. Peter, I would like to see Commissioner Adams before the first of the visitors arrives. Just a word to thank him for his efforts as co-ordinator you know."

"Of course Prime Minister, I'll have a word later today and set something up with your secretary."

"Thank you." The Prime Minister stood up and the other two men rose and gathered their papers together. The Home Secretary shook hands and left but Fox held onto Ainsley's hand for a moment and held him back. The Prime Minister dropped his other hand lightly onto the Foreign Secretary's shoulder.

"Do try to relax a little more Michael. We need you, you know. Or rather I need you. Take things a little easier if you can. I know, don't say it, after the conference. But by then there will be something else to occupy you. Tell me how is Janet? Norma remarked only the other day that we seem to see her only at official functions these days. Why not arrange a little supper party one evening soon? Just the four of us."

"Yes that would be very nice. I'll mention it tonight. But that will definitely be after the conference."

"That I cannot argue with. Goodbye Michael. We'll resume our battles at the meeting on Monday."

"Goodbye Prime Minister."

The Prime Minister walked back to his desk and sat for a moment letting his mind go blank. He was pleased to see that the little trick of relaxation still worked and after a

29

few minutes he picked up his pen and began making marginal notes on the piles of papers before him. A thought crossed his mind and he pressed down the switch on his desk-top intercom.

" Yes sir?"

" Has my wife gone out yet?"

" Yes sir. About five minutes ago, Mrs. Fox is attending the luncheon at the Savoy."

" Yes of course. No matter." He made a note on a pad and tore the sheet off and dropped it into his jacket pocket. The evening would be soon enough but it was important to find any clues he could to the reason for the changes that were so apparent in both the Foreign Secretary and the Home Secretary. He could not quite put his finger on the problem but his wife had an ability to nose out things he could never discover for himself.

*   *   *

Janet Ainsley had picked the dress she was wearing with very great care. Still slim and with her figure showing no signs of the disastrous changes that were blighting many of her friends she was thankful that nature had given her smallish breasts and a metabolism that burned up food rather than turning it to fat. That way her upper body had not sagged and her lower body had not expanded. As far as she could remember she looked the same as she had twenty years before when she had been twenty-one years old and had met and married the up and thrusting politician who had clearly been destined for the great things he had eventually achieved. The only problem that she had now was that just as her body had not altered with the passing years neither had her sexual appetites and that was more than could be said for her husband.

                    *   *   *

She had not consciously set out to have an affair. The need
had been there but was constantly suppressed by a combination of factors. The discretion she was bound to observe
through the loyalty she still felt for her husband. The ever
watchful eyes that were on her most of the time, whether
the eyes of the staff that constantly milled around their
London home or the security men who had been a permanent
part of the entourage of every Cabinet Minister and his
family since the attempt on the life of her husband's predecessor three years before. But the principal reason for the
suppression of her desires had been very basic. Over the past
few years as Michael Ainsley had satisfied her less and less
she had never met any other man for whom she had felt
any attraction. Then she had met John Perring.

                    *   *   *

Perring had walked into her life one morning about six
months before. The security officer assigned to the Foreign
Secretary had been placed on less onerous duties when it was
discovered that he had developed a stomach ulcer that
threatened not only his health but the safety of his charges.
Janet Ainsley had known that a replacement was due to
arrive and she knew his name before they met. Her husband's
secretary had introduced them and on that January morning
they had shaken hands and smiled and said hello and in that
instant Janet had known. Later, when they had been together
in the car and on various formal occasions they had begun
conversations that were at first stilted and tentative and
for a while Janet wondered if she had been attracted to
a man with less than all the confidence she would have expected. Then on a journey back from opening a social centre
in the Midlands she pushed their conversation as far as she

                           31

dared in the chauffeur driven car. That was when Perring had turned and looked at her as they sat together in the back of the car and in his eyes she had seen the unmistakable look. He felt exactly the same about her as she did about him. The diffidence he had shown was only a defence against doing something he dare not do. In that instant she moved her position very slightly in the car so that the chauffeur would see nothing. Her leg had pressed gently against the tall security man and the responding pressure had been quick.

They had not spoken again on that journey but by the time they entered the outskirts of London it had darkened and with the risk gone of the chauffeur seeing anything she had felt his hand take hers. They stayed like that for the final twenty minutes of the journey. Holding hands like, she thought later, two young people from an early more inno- cent age on a first date together. That night had been weeks before and since then there had been no opportunities for talking or touching. But the unspoken messages that passed between them whenever their eyes met seemed at times to Janet Ainsley to be loud enough for everyone to hear.

*   *   *

The previous day the housekeeper at the Ainsley's house in Kent had telephoned. She had to go to stay with her son-in- law while her daughter was in hospital, he was helpless and couldn't look after himself let alone the children and with the builders in working on the extension, the house couldn't be left empty and would Mrs. Ainsley mind. Mrs. Ainsley did not mind. Her husband had scarcely considered the matter. He had enough to think about and if he had ever thought about the security officer who had replaced the earlier man he had certainly not thought of him as rival for his wife's attentions.

32

*   *   *

The dress she had chosen with such care was plain and the colour, a deep red, was one that she knew suited her complexion best. She picked out a heavy, simply patterned gold bracelet and looked at herself in the wardrobe mirror. Her hair was very dark brown lightened by the tiniest glints of red and she wore it slightly longer than she should for her age and position but as she generally looked, and more important felt, years younger than she was she could get away with it. She picked up the light suitcase she had packed, very little was needed as there were many clothes at the house and she duplicated all the essentials of wardrobe and toilet at both houses.

*   *   *

She went down the stairs and Perring was waiting in the hallway with one of her husband's secretarial staff hovering in the background. Perring took the case from her.

"Nothing else Mrs. Ainsley?" She shook her head. "I decided that it was unnecessary for us to take the chauffeur, he would only have to drive back tonight and we shall need a car there. I trust that was in order?" Janet nodded and for an instant the desires she had been concealing for months threatened to overwhelm her. Then she gained control.

"That was the right thing to do. Shall we start? I'll just say good-bye to my husband." She walked through to the Foreign Secretary's ground floor office and looked at him sitting at the desk, the air already thick with cigarette smoke. Ainsley looked up.

"Off?"

"Yes darling. I'll telephone as soon as I arrive. Will you be down at the week-end?"

33

" I don't think so."

" Well if you're not I can come back up. The builders won't be there on Sunday, probably not on Saturday either."

" Well, let's wait and see. The way things are I doubt I shall have any time for several days. Certainly not until after the conference. Oh, by the way, Charles was asking after you. He suggested a supper party, the four of us but after the conference of course."

" Yes that would be nice it's a long time since Norma and I had a gossip." Ainsley stood up and kissed his wife gently on the cheek. Before she was out of the room he was again immersed in his work and he missed the final glance she gave him. Had he seen it he would probably not have interpreted it correctly as the look contained many things. Love and loyalty, guilt and sadness but above all excitement at a prospect that with every minute was becoming less and less endurable.

*　　*

John Perring was not his real name. During the previous ten years he had worked under several names in many countries throughout the world. The jobs he did were seldom of importance. At least not directly. He did not doubt that the men who paid his other, substantial, salary, were getting value for their money but the real purpose of the jobs he did was not always apparent. This one was a little different. A security officer charged with protecting the life of senior government officials and their families seemed likely to have entrée to many things his masters might want. He had found the job surprisingly easy to get.

After the attempt on the life of the former Foreign Secretary in 1975 a high level decision had been taken regarding security measures and these had been expanded to members of opposition parties, leaders from industry, trades union

34

officials and many other prominent figures. Like a lot of other government decisions this one was implemented without regard for the manpower problem it would necessarily impose upon the police and the secret services and the military. A new body had been established welding into a whole, many of the privately operated security forces in the country.

Further recruitment had taken place on a massive scale and Perring had been ordered to apply. His credentials were perfect as indeed they always were and the Australian background that had been created had withstood the scrutiny it had received. Within a few months he had gained the confidence of his superiors as a calm and efficient man and when illness had created the gap on the Foreign Secretary's staff he had asked for and got the job. As bodyguard to the Foreign Secretary's wife he came into fairly regular, if remote contact with many leading figures in government circles and he knew that his monthly reports would have been pleasing to his masters.

Then out of the blue he had received new orders. He had attended several functions as Janet Ainsley's bodyguard and the one at his own country's London embassy had been like all the others but he enjoyed it more for the pleasure in being temporarily on what was, at least technically, his own soil. The man at the bar had started a casual conversation and it was only when no one else was in earshot that he revealed he knew who Perring really was.

" Unorthodox I know but this is urgent and it was felt that face to face was better than trying to put this into writing. You are now guarding the Foreign Secretary's wife."

" Yes, you know that."

" Patience. We want you to exploit that situation more than you are doing."

" How? And why? She doesn't know anything of particular consequence, I've already said that in my reports."

" We know."

35

" Well?"

" It is an order."

" Very well, how?"

" She is an attractive woman for her age. Yes?"

" Yes."

" Have you tried anything?"

" What do you mean?"

" Come now, you know perfectly well what I mean. Your reputation stretches from here to Bangkok, if you will forgive the crudity of my choice of place names. You are envied by many you know."

" I didn't."

" You surprise me. Well? Have you tried anything?"

" No."

" Sure?"

" Of course."

" What about her? Has she said anything to suggest she finds you attractive."

" What is all this leading to?"

" Answer the question. I really am surprised to find you so coy. Your reputation doesn't say that about you."

" Yes I think she has noticed me."

" Good. And I am inclined to think that your reluctance to answer my questions stems from the fact that you would like to return that attention."

" Now wait . . ."

" No you wait. Don't get upset. It is good if this is so. It makes what we want you to do that much easier."

" Well?"

" We want you to have an affair with the lady in question."

" What?"

" Really my friend, with every moment you are becoming less like the person you are supposed to be. We want you to seduce her." Perring had stared at the other man who had turned to gaze casually at the throng of distinguished people milling around the room. He followed the man's eyes and he saw Janet Ainsley and he felt his mouth go dry.

"But why? Alright I know it's an order but it seems senseless."

"Perhaps. There are other things besides information you know. Blackmail and other pressures."

"When?"

"When? As soon as possible, as to where and how I leave that in your capable hands. I am certain you will find a way."

"What about reports, any changes?"

"No, everything as usual. I'll say goodnight then." The man had smiled and drifted away into another room and Perring had stood there, stunned. He had done as he had been told of course.

Indeed it had been all too easy. A few days after the meeting at the embassy he had accompanied Janet Ainsley out of town and on the way back he had been surprised to find her making a move that suggested she was more than eager to enter into a very different relationship to the one they had had until then. At first it had proved awkward, they had very few moments when they were alone and there were a few signs in both of them of the frustrations they were feeling. Then the trip to Kent had come about and when it did he knew that at last he was going to do what he had been ordered to do. That was when he became aware of something he had not noticed before. His feelings towards the woman. They were quite unlike the feelings he had experienced before with all the others. It made him feel uncertain. Not that he lacked confidence in his relationships with any woman. Quite the reverse in fact. He had never developed a lasting relationship with anyone for the dictates of his work kept him moving so much and he could not permit the prying that seemed to follow inevitably upon the blossoming of an initial purely sexual attraction. His affairs had always been brief and usually very exhausting, physically if not emotionally and without exception they had been with women ten or more years younger than his thirty-five. Janet Ainsley was a very different matter.

* * *

From the start he had been aware of her physical attractiveness. Any man would have been. Her dress sense had at first seemed a little old-fashioned and her manner had been very restrained.

Gradually over the months he had known her that had changed. The way she dressed was the first thing to alter and he now realised that the manner of her dress before was simply to remain in keeping with the position she held as the Foreign Secretary's wife. He now guessed rightly that he was the reason for the changes she had made. He was sure that the slightly shorter dresses, the styles of dress that showed her excellent figure to better advantage, were all done subconsciously in the beginning. And her manner towards him, changing from the cool, distant attitude of her initial reaction to the warmer, friendlier and latterly overtly provocative air was also initially done without conscious thought.

* * *

Even before the contact at the embassy he had felt attracted by her but he had held himself back. Partly because he was uncertain how his masters would have reacted and partly out of the simple caution shown by any man thrown together with a married woman, particularly one in the public eye. He decided that the affair with Janet Ainsley would be interesting, different because of the strange circumstances. He decided he would enjoy it even though it would probably prove unmemorable.

*　　*　　*

He tried to find a connection between his new instructions and those he had received in the April of that same year. They had told him to await an outside contact in July and to do whatever he was asked. As contact for a Sleeper in the United Kingdom he assumed the outsider and the Sleeper were planning to meet and would be using him as a go-between. He was wrong in that assumption but he was right when he further assumed his stay in England was coming to an end. Once he had been used he moved on. That was standard procedure to prevent accidental uncovering of a Sleeper. This time he would be sorry to go. He was wrong although he did not yet know it in his assessment of his relationship with Janet Ainsley.

*　　*　　*

They had not felt like eating lunch on the way down to the house in Kent but they had stopped nonetheless because they knew the builders would be at the house until the light failed and as that meant eight o'clock or later they decided by unspoken agreement that the less time spent in the house with others present the better. Sitting close together in the car and in the restaurant at the little pub where they picked at their food was difficult because they could not risk the tiniest sign of their real feelings. In the house it would have been unendurable.

Even so they were still at the house by mid-afternoon and both of them occupied the time as best they could. After she had telephoned her husband to dutifully report her safe arrival Janet had toured the house looking for jobs to do. She spent a long time in her bedroom.

*   *   *

Perring spent the first hour doing his official job. He thoroughly checked out the house and grounds. Then he watched the builders at work until their irritable looks sent him elsewhere. He had noted the position of all the telephones in the house and he waited until he could hear by her movements that Janet was not near one of the other instruments. Then he called the answering service that monitored one of two telephones at his flat, during his frequent absences. There were no messages for him and they noted the number where he could be contacted. The number of that particular telephone was ex-directory and apart from the answering service the only people who knew the number were his masters who did not make contact that way, the Sleeper in case of emergency and anyone to whom his masters gave the number. He knew they would have given it only to the man who was to make contact with him. After that was done he sat and waited wondering idly if the contact was for a harmless reason or one likely to cause a major incident. Some of the contacts he had been involved with had ended rather messily and he found himself hoping this one would not be like that.

*   *   *

Eventually Janet came into the room and sat opposite him and they waited together with their tensions and desires mounting to bursting point as the builders eventually decided they had done all they could in the light that remained and slowly packed up work for the day.

Her husband apart, Janet Ainsley had been intimate with only one man. That had been a single occasion with a man she scarcely knew about two years before she had met

40

Michael Ainsley. The aftermath of a university dance had taken its toll of a lot of things apart from her natural reluctance to give herself to any man outside the marriage she hoped to make at some future date. The effect of the dancing and drinking and the heat had worn away her resolve and the morning found her in bed with the man and with almost no recollection of how or even what had happened. She had got out of bed and dressed and she had left quietly and she never saw him again. When she met Michael Ainsley a few months later she knew she had found the man she was to marry and she never mentioned the subject of her single straying from an otherwise flawless path. Neither did she think about it again until that warm July evening when she sat with John Perring listening to the builders men drive away from the house. There was no similarity in the two occasions and she was annoyed that her subconscious should have dredged up the old affair. There was no real comparison.

Her life with Ainsley had been precisely what she had wanted. An attractive older man and an ambitious one who had become the youngest Foreign Secretary of modern times and she had done much to help and support him both in and out of office. But there had been a cost. The gradual disintegration of their private life had been so slow that for months she had fought against acceptance that all was not well. A lot of Ainsley's coolness she knew lay in the pace at which he was obliged to work. The travelling and the long hours and the overseas trips all eroded the time they could spend together and similarly their closeness when they were alone.

Recently the number of times they made love had fallen to once every few months and then it was so unsatisfactory as to be, in any other circumstances, laughable. She was not sure of her feelings for Perring. She knew that in many senses she still loved her husband but in the sexual sense she felt nothing for him and everything for the tall, handsome

41

tough-looking man who had come into her life as her body-guard.

*   *   *

Unable to wait any longer she stood up and walked over to him. " They've gone," she said feeling very slightly embar-rassed both at the foolishness of her words and at the im-plied openness of the invitation. Perring stood and looked down at her. He smiled slightly and walked over to draw the heavy curtains at the window that looked out over the garden at the rear of the house. He turned back to her.

" I think a drink would be a good idea."

" No."

" Yes. We're both too tense. We want everything to be right. Let's relax, just for a while." He poured two drinks and she noted even in that moment that he had control of the situation. Her drink was a large one, his was very small and well weakened with soda.

" I feel like a young girl on her first date. It's silly."

" No it isn't silly. And you look like a young girl, I'm not sure about the first date part though. You probably have the better of me in experience."

" Why do you think I make a habit of this . . . this kind of thing?"

She turned away abruptly angry with him.

" No Janet my love I didn't mean that. You know I didn't but you are a very beautiful woman and the world is full of men who would give a great deal to be where I am now."

" There was only one man apart from my husband and that was only once and it was before I met Michael. As for Michael. He is less than what I imagine a good lover should be and recently he has been . . . well . . . even less responsive than usual."

" He's a busy man."

42

" You don't have to make excuses for him you know."

" And we don't have to fight."

" I'm sorry John. I'm, I'm nervous." Perring walked over and took the glass from her hand. He stood both glasses on the low coffee table and then put his arms around her and kissed her once almost chastely and instantly she responded and kissed him back with a savagery that surprised him. For a few moments longer part of his brain stood apart and considered the situation then without conscious thought he set aside any qualm he felt at what he was doing. Subconsciously his desire had blotted out the fear he felt that his masters might find out what was happening to him.

" Let's go upstairs. Now." He nodded agreement and started to follow her to the stairs.

" You go up. I'd better earn my pay and lock everywhere." He locked and bolted the doors and checked all the windows before he picked up the whisky bottle and their glasses and carried them up the stairs to the bedroom from where he could see a soft light gleaming.

*　　*　　*

In the few minutes she had been alone Janet Ainsley had set aside any further thoughts she still harboured that might prevent her from enjoying to the full what was about to happen. She stood in the centre of the large low ceilinged room waiting for him. When he came into the bedroom he stopped at the door for an instant before stepping inside to push the door closed with his foot. He walked over to the bed and stood the bottle and glasses on the bedside table and then he looked at her again. He had decided long ago that she was very probably the loveliest woman he had ever known and he felt the desire that had been growing for weeks rise towards exploding point. He walked towards her and taking her face between his hands he kissed her gently as he

43

had done earlier downstairs. He had already noted with the careful planning of an experienced predator that her dress had a simple zip-fastening at the back and he released it and drew it smoothly down. He felt the dress slip away to the ground between their feet and as his hands caressed her back he was surprised and pleased to find she was not wearing a bra. Nine times out of ten, for all his experience with them, he found their fastenings not particularly conducive to the smooth removal he had achieved with the dress and he mentally applauded her foresight. He bent his head and slowly ran his lips over her shoulders and down to brush against her nipples. He found them erect as he had expected and he sucked gently at them for a moment before dropping to his knees to run his tongue dartingly over her stomach and down to her inner thighs. He felt her trembling and quite suddenly he was no longer in calm control as he had intended being. He wanted her and he wanted her then and quickly.

*   *   *

He rose to his feet lifting her as he did so and half pulled, half carried her to the bed. Her hands joined his in removing his clothes and pulling away the tiny briefs she still wore. For an instant his fingers touched her to ensure she was ready for him and swiftly and urgently he entered her. For only seconds their bodies thrust and jerked at each other and then it was over. He rolled sideways and for the first time he could remember he felt guilty.

" Janet I'm sorry. I didn't plan on it being that way. I was going to take time. All night. Not that way, like an adolescent."

" It's alright. I wanted it that way. More than that I needed it. And we still have all night. With nothing to interrupt us." She sat up and looked down at him in the growing darkness that was filling the room. She pulled back the covers on the bed and slid inside. After a moment he followed her and they closed their arms around each other and kissed again but this time there was an intensity in Janet Ainsley's kiss that even exceeded what had passed before. Perring was slowly getting over his annoyance at himself for not taking time as he was accustomed to doing but with Janet's kiss he began to worry again. He was not sufficiently sure of his ground to want the relationship to develop too far. It would make it all that more difficult when inevitably they had to part. He reached over to the side table and poured them both a drink. For once he gave himself a drink as big as the one he gave her. Having failed to maintain his control the first time there wasn't very much he had to lose.

" Where do you come from?"

" What?" The question was not all that unexpected. Sooner or later it happened with every woman he associated with. It was surprising the question had not been asked before but then this was the first occasion they had been completely alone. Inevitably being a woman, Janet would have built up an array of questions for him but, unlike the other women he had from time to time, it would not be easy to fob her off with half answers or even to adopt the slightly mysterious attitude he found worked well with some younger women. He would have to be careful.

" I asked where do you come from?"

" Do you mean where do I live or where was I born and bred?"

" Both."

" Well, first things first. I was born in Birmingham." He waited. He usually used Birmingham as it was a big place and allowed him room to manoeuvre. If the person he was speaking to said they too came from there or asked the district he had a choice of several over a wide enough area to avoid being asked details. If pressed lightly he had been to Birmingham two or three times and could usually manage a vague discussion about the place. If the questioning grew too close he could easily step aside by saying that although born there he had left at an early age and couldn't really remember much about it. Janet Ainsley said nothing so he went on.

"We all moved to Australia a few years ago. Well more than a few really. I was nineteen and I only went to help my mother and father settle in with the younger kids. I planned on coming back after a year or so. But then after we'd been there six months my dad died and I decided to stay. I came back here a few years ago."

He waited again but there was still no response and he wondered for a moment if the woman beside him was asleep.

"And where do you live now?" So she wasn't asleep but she had bought the first part of the story. The second part was less easy. He knew that if she really wanted to do so she could find his address and call at the flat. That would be intolerable. He could not permit a visit to the flat where the unlisted telephone might ring and be answered unwittingly by the wife of the Secretary of State for Foreign Affairs.

"Chelsea," he said and waited. She did not ask where, precisely, in Chelsea he lived and he breathed a little more easily. She was too mature to pursue the point he thought and even if she did know the address he hoped she would not be foolish enough to visit him there.

*   *   *

He looked at the woman beside him and was relieved to see that she was sleeping quietly. He let his thoughts drift back over the afternoon's events. Giving the answering service the number of the Foreign Secretary's country house had been foolish. He should not have done it, he should have chanced being unobtainable but it was too late and he could not undo it. Hopefully there would be no call that day. Or the following two days. On Sunday they would be on their way back or even earlier if he could arrange it. He toyed with the idea of inventing a reason for not staying even that one night but then he felt Janet's fingers stroking gently against his thigh. She was not asleep after all. He began to respond and quickly the mounting desire thrust aside the worries about the possibility of the call coming that weekend. He turned towards her and this time with complete control began to make love to her in a way he was sure would be an entirely new experience for her.

*   *   *

It was. Janet Ainsley had meant what she had said when earlier they had both climaxed so quickly but she could not honestly say that she had expected anything else. Her experience with Michael had never given her anything other than brief couplings usually started too soon and over too quickly, at least for her. This second time with Perring was a revelation of something she had never dreamed would exist for her. His hands manipulated gently but firmly every part of her body until she felt as if every nerve was attuned only to him. When he came into her that second time it was perfect. And surprisingly it was perfect for John Perring too and afterwards as they lay there, this time close and warm in bed, he began to wonder if there might be some way out. Some way he could continue to serve his masters and at the same time keep this woman. He never gave even mental voice to the word but for the first time in his life John Perring was giving way to something that had caused the death of too many of his colleagues in the dangerous field in which he operated. He was falling in love.

When the telephone rang it brought him back to reality with a savagery he felt to his toes. He knew it was for him. Fate was not letting him get away with it. Janet answered the call

47

on the telephone that stood on the small table on the landing outside the bedroom. She called him to the door.

" It's for you. It's your answering service. Must you answer it?" He did not answer and avoided looking into her eyes as he took the instrument from her.

" Yes?"

" Mr. Perring? Sorry to disturb you but we had a call from a gentleman. He was most insistent that we contact you and tell you he wants to speak to you urgently. He was calling from a kiosk and said he would call us back in about half an hour. I'm afraid he wouldn't give his name. He said you would know who it was."

" Yes. Thank you. When he calls back please give him this number." He hung up and turned away. Janet was standing in the doorway to the bedroom. Silhouetted against the light from the bedside table she looked more desirable than ever before but for Perring she might have been made of stone.

" John what is it?"

" A small problem. One of the men in my division has had an accident. The head of the division wants to speak to me urgently. He'll be calling here in a moment." She turned and walked back to the bed and he followed and poured them both a drink this time making his a very small one.

" John?" He detected the questioning tone in her voice and was instantly on guard.

" Yes?"

" Why had your chief to go through your answering service? Surely he knows where you are!" He cursed himself for the childish error.

He thought quickly.

" Well you of all people should know about government departments. No one ever knows what the other man is doing." Janet nodded and seemed to forget the matter.

*   *   *

48

When the telephone rang again he was waiting. He did not recognise the voice. At the other end of the telephone line Stellman gave his instructions quietly in his very ordinary voice. But the things he wanted Perring to do were very far from ordinary.

THREE

Stellman found the waitress's room with very little difficulty. Although he always avoided speaking unnecessarily to people he was aware that extremes of silence were more likely to draw attention than being loquacious. He had talked easily and naturally to the girl as she had taken his order and as each course was served.

It was while she served his coffee that she had remarked that she was pleased her shift was nearly over and she would be glad " to put her feet up." He had casually asked if she had far to go to get home and she had cheerfully volunteered that she lived on the premises. When he returned to the motel he found the living quarters easily enough. At that time in the morning he knew people's reactions were at a very low ebb and he decided to risk opening the doors of all the staff bedrooms. He was lucky, the girl was in the second one he tried, but another girl shared the room. He waited outside the window for only five minutes when he heard a light ring from an alarm clock inside the room. He heard one girl moving about and washing at a basin in the corner of the room. He stepped quietly back into the corridor in time to see the room door open. The girl who came out was not his waitress.

He was inside the room before the other girl was out of sight. He awakened his waitress very gently and he quickly calmed her from the first moment of fear.

" Have they asked about me?" He didn't have to tell her he referred to the police.

" Yes sir."

" What did you tell them."

" They asked me to describe what you looked like. How you spoke. That's all."

" What about pictures. Have they made one up from your description?"

" No sir. The Inspector, Mr. Walters, he's getting a Photo-Fit he called it. We're going to do that this morning."

" I see." He thought for a moment. " Thank you, what is your name?"

" Jenny sir, Jenny Franklin."

" Thank you Jenny. That's all I wanted to know. Do whatever they ask you to do won't you? You must help the police." He felt the girl relax at the unexpected remark and that was the moment when he swept up the pillow from under her head and over on to her face in one smooth movement. Her struggles were fierce but that moment's advantage he had given himself was sufficient. He held the pillow there until she had stopped moving. Then he counted slowly to two hundred before he lifted the pillow. The girl's eyes were open and in death her slightly cheap prettiness had changed to a gawky ugliness. He left the room as quietly as he had entered and in a few minutes he reached the car he had left a little way from the motel entrance.

*　　*　　*

Harry Walters was alone for the first time since it had happened. He allowed himself the luxury of holding his head in his hands and cursing softly, half under his breath. The object of his attack was himself. Logically he could not really hold himself to blame for what had happened, but that was not a time for logical thought to come easily.

*   *   *

The nightmare had begun when he had caught a glimpse of one of the other waitresses, the one he knew shared a room with the girl who had waited on the missing guest, and he had called over to her.

" Is Miss Franklin still sleeping?"

" Yes. All the excitement I suppose. I left her there. An extra half hour will have helped. Do you want her now?"

" Yes. I think we had better make a start. Would you mind calling her?" The girl went off down the corridor that led to the staff quarters at the rear of the main building. He started to clear a space on the table he was using ready to help the girl build up the Photo-Fit picture when he heard the footsteps coming down the corridor. Someone was running and running fast.

Sensing trouble he crossed the room to open the door before the steps reached it. It was the waitress. She was out of breath and from the look of horror on her face he knew she would not be able to speak for minutes. In that same instant he knew what had happened. He sprinted down the corridor and reached the open door to the girl's room. He stopped and looked at the still figure on the bed.

Slowly and carefully he stepped the short distance to the bed and reached down to rest a finger against the girl's neck. There was no sign of a pulse. He looked into the open dead eyes for a long moment and then moved slowly backwards to the door following the path he had used coming in to the room. He heard the approach of the detective constable without turning round. He reached forward and gently closed the door.

" Stay here. No one in. No one unless I'm here. Right?"

He went back to the small office. The waitress was sobbing harshly and two of the motel's male staff were trying clumsily to console her and obviously neither knew what had caused her to act in that way. He sent one of the two men in search of a woman staff member. He looked down at the girl and took a deep breath.

" I'm sorry, I have to ask you some questions. Okay?" The girl nodded. " No doubt she was alive when you left the room this morning. Did she speak or anything?"

" No." The voice was almost inaudible and he had to lean forward to hear the words. " She didn't speak. But she was alright. The cover had slipped off the bed and I pulled it up over her. She didn't wake up but she turned over and was laying on her back when I came out."

" Did you see anyone? Anyone apart from people who work here?"

" No. I didn't see anyone until I went into the kitchen. Some of the other girls were there and we had a cup of tea and a chat and then I came out and you called to me."

" Fine. Okay. That's fine." He had heard a tapping at the door and had looked up with relief to see one of the other waitresses. He was glad to see she was older and seemed calm and capable. He let her lead the younger woman away and then reached for the telephone. As soon as the murder team were on their way he went out and down the corridor to the manager's office. The manager was standing at the door trying to maintain an air of indifference to what was going on around him. Walters kept moving and the other man backed into the room and sat at his desk.

" No one in that part of the building. Understand. No one. Keep everyone here. Staff members that is. If any are due to go off duty keep them here. Guests too. They stay. There will be some uniformed police here in a few minutes and they will prevent anyone from leaving. Until then it's up to you and me. Right? Get moving then."

"Jenny. Jenny Franklin. It's her isn't it? What has happened?"

"She's dead."

"Jesus."

"Now get going." Walters' tone had softened at the man's obvious distress. "Just carry on normally but see no one slips out before the uniformed boys arrive. Right? Yell for me if you have any bother." The manager hurried away and Walters went on down the corridor. As he passed the door to the kitchen he glanced in through the glass pane and saw a heavily built man he recognised from the previous night's interviews. He pushed open the door and went in.

"Mr. Parsons, isn't it? You're the handyman."

"That's right sir. Is it true? Has some bastard killed young Jenny?"

"Looks like it Mr. Parsons. I need some help for a few minutes until more men arrive."

"Anything you like." Parsons followed him down to the girls' room.

"Now stay here. No one goes in. No one even so much as touches the door. Right?" He knew he was taking a risk. The book that would probably be thrown at him for a murder being committed under his nose would be heavy enough without using a possible suspect as a guard on the murder room. But he had to try to get an identification on the vehicle the missing man from room nine had used. The previous night's questioning had failed to turn up anyone who had noticed the car. With a night's sleep there was a chance, however slim, that someone's memory had improved. He and the d.c. had swiftly and systematically begun to run through the staff and remaining guests. Halfway through, the first car had arrived and he had co-opted one of the uniformed constables onto the small enquiry team, the other taking over from Parsons.

53

*　　*　　*

Shortly after the first car the second had arrived with Superintendent Macrae and Detective Sergeant Norris. He had
taken the superintendent aside to brief him on the interest
taken in the case by the Metropolitan Police Commissioner
and the Americans who were on their way to the motel.
Macrae was immediately alert to the fact that Walters was
likely to have the combined wrath of several powerful men
descend upon him and also at the need for special care in
what was clearly something more than a simple murder case.
He trod lightly on Walters' part in the matter and told his
team who had started to arrive in dribs and drabs to take
even more than their customary care.

*　　*　　*

He left Harry Walters to the task of assessing the result of
questioning all the guests about the car driven by the missing
man. That didn't take long. One man had arrived at about
the same time and thought the car was dark in colour and
might have been a Cortina or a Vauxhall but he wasn't sure
as all modern cars looked alike, didn't they? Privately, Harry
Walters had agreed. He tried to recall how often that or a
similar phrase had found its way into his notebook. There
was the usual stereotyped remark about foreigners in there,
didn't all blacks/Chinese/Indians look alike?

Lately the stereotype remarks had moved on to encompass
anyone who wasn't typically English (whatever that meant)
and everyone who wore a uniform. But the disease had
spread, the long, male hairstyles of the late sixties and early
seventies had left behind them a rash of identifications that
were not even certain of the sex of the person under enquiry,
all young people looked alike didn't they?

Then generalisations had begun to appear in his notebook. All blacks/Chinese/Indians were shiftless and couldn't be trusted. All men in uniform apart from looking alike were incipient dictators. And as for all policemen, what were they not? He had lost count of the number of times he had been accused, subtly by the public and overtly by the press and by defending counsel, of being either a fool or a liar or both. The number of times that had happened was probably about the same as the number of times he felt like quitting. But he never did, even when his marriage had crumbled around him.

*　　*　　*

Pamela, his wife, had said it was because of the job. He told himself at the time that she had wanted an excuse that wouldn't hurt him too much, that really it was him not the job that was at fault. But in the three years that had followed the divorce he had come to believe that she had been speaking the truth. Since the divorce he had become more introspective. He spent the few nights he was not working thinking and that only made matters worse. His marriage had lasted two and a half years and in retrospect it seemed a miracle it had lasted that long.

Not just the hours although they were bad enough, but the changes it had brought about in him. A hardening, a ruthlessness, a lack of feeling for the subtleties of life with Pamela. Then it had all gone, gone because he lived and breathed the job. Everything he did was work, at times he felt like the spider he had read about, where the male was eaten alive by the female as soon as it had fertilised her eggs, sometimes even as it was doing so. Only with him the female spider was the job. It sucked him dry and he knew it was doing it and he could do nothing to stop it, he couldn't even walk away.

Knowing he wasn't alone hadn't helped. For every police

officer with the same kind of problems he knew dozens who, somehow, had made the adjustment. Privately he thought they had compromised somewhere along the line. They couldn't lead normal lives and at the same time bring to the job the burning devotion he did. And every time he thought that, he knew he was wrong about that too. There wasn't an easy answer if there was an answer at all. Occasionally when he reached that stage of thinking he allowed himself a few moments of luxurious self-pity and he did so then.

" Harry." The Superintendent put his head round the door.

" Yes sir."

" The Americans you were expecting are here. At least there's a Cadillac outside with a flag on the bonnet." Walters went out into the lobby of the motel. The two men who climbed out of the long black embassy car were very different. One was tall and could not have been mistaken for anything other than an American and a military American at that. That had to be Colonel Hunt. The other man was small and very dark. He would be Comoy. Comoy looked around at the police cars and turned towards the two men waiting to greet him. Walters stepped forward and introduced himself and Macrae. Comoy looked questioningly at the Superintendent and turned to Walters.

" I thought you were in charge here Inspector. Has something else happened?"

" Yes sir, I'm afraid it has."

" The girl?" The words were more than just a question, they were also a flat statement of fact. And there was something else in the small man's tone. A resigned acceptance of the inevitable.

" She's dead. Probably murdered. We'll know in a minute or so. The doctor's in there now."

" I see. I take it you are now in charge Superintendent."

" That's correct Mr. Comoy. I understand from what Mr.

Walters has been telling me there is more to this than a routine robbery and a routine murder."

"Very much so. As Commissioner Adams told Mr. Walters last night, you can be sure the missing man had nothing to do with your robberies. Equally I am sure that he had everything to do with the waitress's death."

"Did you talk to the girl last night?" The American Colonel spoke for the first time and Walters wondered what position Comoy must hold to have the authority to take charge, as he clearly had over a colonel.

"I have a description of the man and of the way he spoke."

"What about an Identikit picture?"

"No sir. We were to do that this morning. From the way the girl talked I think it would have been a good likeness. It would have been a Photo-Fit as well, we don't use Identikit any more."

"Damn it." The colonel swore softly and lapsed into silence again.

"I take it no one else saw enough of him to help us," Comoy asked.

"No. He spoke to the receptionist who didn't look at his face and can't remember what his voice was like except that he spoke quietly. He was alone in the dining room and therefore only Jenny Franklin saw him close to."

"I see. We'd better have the description the girl, Miss Franklin, gave you. At least it's a start." Walters led the way into the small office and the two Americans followed. Macrae excused himself and went back down the corridor towards the murder room.

"What about the car he used. Any description of that?"

"Nothing of any use Colonel. Dark colour, could be a Ford Cortina or a Vauxhall Victor but from the vagueness of the man who saw it it could easily be something else."

"So there are no road blocks up?"

"No sir. No point." Walters thought for a moment and then tentatively asked. "This man, obviously you want him. Have you another description or a photograph? It might help to jog memories." Comoy looked at the inspector and there was an indefinable expression in his almost black eyes.

"No there isn't. As far as we know the only person who could help us is the dead girl. Now all we have is the description in your note book."

Walters resisted the almost overpowering impulse to ask another question but he sensed that a request for an explanation would meet with a refusal. He picked up the girl's statement.

"This is what she said. 'He was very quiet. He spoke softly and I had to strain to hear him. He had a bit of an accent but I don't know what it was. He wasn't very tall. I'm five-five in the shoes I wear for work and he was only about three or four inches taller than me. He was ordinary looking. His hair was sandyish, not real ginger more fair. He was very sunburned as if he'd just come back from his holidays. His eyes were blue. I didn't notice any marks on his face or hands, you know scars or things. He was quiet. Have I said that? I don't mean just that he didn't say much. He was, well, restful if you know what I mean.'" Walters dropped the paper to the desk in front of Comoy who read the statement through carefully. There was a long silence.

"I'd like to copy this down Inspector."

"Yes sir of course." Walters pulled a sheet of paper across the desk and watched as the American carefully copied the statement the girl had made. He had just finished when the door opened and Macrae walked in.

"The doctor is just leaving. He reckons suffocation with the pillow. Do either of you gentlemen want to talk to him?"

"No I don't think so. Thank you Superintendent." The door swung to behind Macrae and there was silence until he came back after letting the doctor get away.

" Can I use the telephone?" Comoy asked.

" Of course," Walters pushed the telephone across the desk and watched in silence as the other man dialled a number he took from a small note-book.

" Commissioner Adams please. Lewis Comoy." This time the silence that fell was tense as if the two police officers were unconsciously stiffening at the impending presence of a senior officer.

" Commissioner? Comoy. Problems I'm afraid. The girl is dead. Murdered. No, frankly I think there is nothing to be gained by us staying here. There is something I want to talk to you about. I will have to go back to the Embassy first and call Washington. After that can I come over and see you? Sometime this afternoon. Okay." He replaced the receiver and stared at the copy he had made of the girl's statement. He looked up at Macrae.

" Can I ask you to keep me informed on your investigations. Anything at all. Routine reports, the lot. If there are any problems please ask your Chief Constable to talk to Mr. Adams. He'll reassure him that this is a matter of very great importance." He glanced sideways at Walters. " Don't feel too bad about it Inspector. You weren't to expect this happening. No one could have expected it." The words did very little to alleviate Walters' feeling of gloom and apart from anything else he had a distinct feeling that if he had known more about the man, as much perhaps as Comoy did, he might have acted differently.

*   *   *

The same thought was in Comoy's mind as the Embassy car slid out of the motel entrance and turned towards London. He stared at the back of the driver's neck and tried to enumerate the possible reasons for the man being in England. There were dozens but one seemed to be more likely than the others.

"Why are you contacting Washington?" the colonel asked.

"Two reasons, one is to tell them about the print and the second is to recommend that the President does not attend the conference."

"Telling them about the print will stir up a hornets' nest, no doubt about that, but I don't know that you should offer that particular piece of advice to the President."

"Frank. When Leeson gets to London it's up to me to see that he is safe at all times. The job was about as routine as this kind of thing can be until Inspector Walters turned up that fingerprint. Now it's anything but routine. We have a grade one problem and the easiest answer is for the President to stay away."

"Maybe, but David Leeson is not a man who takes advice easily. He won't love you for it."

"I don't want him to love me for it. I want him to avoid taking unnecessary risks."

"He won't see it as an unnecessary risk. This meeting is an important one you know."

"I know. I also know that it is coming at a time when all the major powers are smiling at one another for a change. That means their guards will be down. That makes it all the more risky. He should stay away. Say he's ill. Ask for a postponement. Give us more time. Change the venue quickly. Any damn thing to give us an edge."

"Suit yourself, Lewis, but I don't think he'll listen to you." Comoy sank lower into the cushioned seat of the Cadillac. He knew perfectly well the President would not take any heed of the advice he meant to send. He also knew that in sending it he would risk Washington asking if he was really up to the job. He wondered if he was. His near-obsession had lain dormant for a lot of years until the call from Commissioner Adams had re-awakened all the old fears and anger. He closed his eyes and feigned sleep. It was one way to avoid further conversation with Hunt. But he didn't sleep and he had a feeling he was not going to sleep very much at all for the next few days.

*　　*　　*

Stellman had already decided to change the car. As far as he knew the Cortina had not been observed apart from the guest who had arrived at the motel about the same time. He might have remembered the make and the colour but certainly not the registration number. Nevertheless he was not taking that risk. Not after what he had just done. He drove on down the A3 towards Portsmouth. That would be as good a place as any to change cars. It would also be a good place from where to telephone the contact. It was time to start preparing for the job.

*　　*　　*

At the motel there had been a subtle shift in authority. Macrae had talked to the Chief Constable who had talked to Commissioner Adams and the Chief Constable had then called back to Macrae. Every report had to be duplicated and sent to the Met. That irritated Macrae but he had accepted that there was a lot more to the girl's death than met the eye. The robbery investigation had almost stopped. Every available man except one had been pulled off onto the murder enquiry. The exception was Harry Walters who stayed on the robbery investigation with the feeling of a man about to be pushed off the end of a plank into a shark-infested sea. What was worse was not knowing why it was all happening to him.

*　　*　　*

It was mid-afternoon before Comoy had finished talking to Washington and there was no doubt that Frank Hunt's remark about stirring up a hornet's nest was justified. The incredulous noises that came down the line proved that. And there was equally no doubt that his recommendations to the President were not approved but his reputation in the Department was enough to ensure that the message would be passed on although very probably accompanied by one suggesting the President should ignore his. He also asked permission to do something else, something Washington only agreed to after a long argument.

*　　*　　*

Stellman was beginning to feel irritable. Normally he found the elaborate steps he took to avoid leaving a trail, before and after a job, enjoyable. Partly because they allowed him to be active without risk and to keep his mind occupied with trivia and thus free from worrying over the details of what had to follow. But this time he was bored by it all. He should have been settled in the motel in Surrey. He should have stayed there quietly with the freedom to develop his arrangements with the contact. Instead he was still driving, he had no base and he found the heavy traffic of the English roads difficult after the almost empty roads of the island where he made his home. In Portsmouth he arranged garaging for his Cortina. The story he told was simple enough. He was going away by boat on business and he would be back in six weeks. That would give Carter ample time to collect the car and return it to Godfrey Davis at Gatwick. He hired the third car in two days, this time from Avis using the same name and licence as for the other two and headed back towards London in another Cortina, this time a white one. He stayed on the main road for a few miles before turning off to follow a north-westerly route to avoid passing

62

the area close to the motel. He decided to find a hotel before trying to reach his contact. It was early evening before he found a small quiet hotel on the outskirts of Reading that seemed suitable. He washed and shaved and had a meal served in his room. He wanted no more close contact with waitresses.

After he had eaten he went out on foot. He walked about half a mile before he found a telephone kiosk. When he was answered by an answering service he felt the irritations of the day building up inside him particularly when they refused to give him the number where the man calling himself Perring could be located. After a coldly angry exchange he walked on down the road and about half an hour later he came to another telephone. That time the answering service gave him a number and he planted it deep into his retentive memory.

Then he called the number and spoke to the man called Perring. Perring said very little but what he did say was in a tone that did not sit too well in Stellman's subconscious. There was something about it that he did not like. It was some time before he was able to define it satisfactorily. A combination of fear and resentment. Stellman was concerned. Not at Perring's emotions. What concerned him was that while a frightened man could be useful, provided he maintained control, a resentful man was a very different matter That could be dangerous particularly during the period before the job when Stellman needed him the most.

When he went to bed that night he lay awake for almost an hour before he slept but when he did it was a dreamless and completely relaxed sleep. As if he had no cares at all in the world.

*　　*　　*

The meeting between Lewis Comoy and Raymond Adams had

been delayed until the evening. The Commissioner had been under severe pressure for several days and the complete loss of sleep the previous night had left him feeling far from his best. He had called the American Embassy and told Comoy he wanted a couple of hours sleep. Comoy understood and that understanding made itself apparent even over the telephone. Whatever Comoy's duties really were Adams knew he was a professional with a professional's understanding of the problems that beset their fellows all over the world.

*   *   *

He telephoned his wife and made the standard excuse that had developed over the years into a half-joking ritual. There was never a complaint. Adams reflected over his marriage after he had made the call and was washing and shaving at the small washbasin fitted into the tiny ante-room adjoining his office. He had met his wife when he was still a detective inspector. Hard-working and exceptionally good at the job, he had made no secret of his ambitions to Muriel Grey when they had met when he was questioning a patient at the hospital where she was a nurse. Their courtship had been erratic, filled with broken dates from both sides as duty called them.

They had decided against children at a time when to do so was unfashionable and regarded in their community as slightly odd. Over the years their off-duty periods had seldom blended well and in idle moments they calculated that they probably spent less than a third of the time together than the average couple in their age group. It didn't seem to matter. They were very happy and they enjoyed a deep love and respect for each other and for each other's career. Adams finished at the wash basin and stretched out on the long endless settee that filled one wall of the ante-room. The settee had long since ceased to be a joke and had become instead a much needed asset to the incumbent of the office. He let

64

himself drift into a half-sleep still thinking about his wife. He smiled as he dozed.

*   *   *

The telephone rang and he wakened quickly and was instantly alert. He stood up and went through into the office. The switchboard girl told him he had had the two hours respite from calls he had asked for. He told the girl to get the American Embassy for him and in moments he was talking again to Comoy. He spent the thirty minutes the American took to arrive by eating a pile of eggs, steak and potatoes that would have gladdened the heart of any self-respecting heavy-weight boxer and he topped it off with the entire contents of the large teapot the canteen kept especially for the Commissioner's known habits. He was as fresh and alert as if he had been on a weekend's leave when Comoy was shown into the office.

" Well Mr. Comoy, we seem to have had a problem or two down in Surrey. Your man turned out to be rather dangerous."

" Yes he is Commissioner. I should have said more than I did but there were several reasons why I did not, could not. Apart from anything else I . . . look this is a very complicated business. I've been talking to Washington and among other things I asked permission to brief you fully. They gave me that permission. After a lot of sweat I might add." Adams leaned forward and rested his chin on a steeple of fingers.

" Would it help if I knew just who you are?" Comoy grinned.

" Yes, sorry about that. I have the habit of secrecy. I'm with a special services division of the U.S. government. Not the C.I.A. not the F.B.I. A completely separate unit answerable only to four men. The President, the Vice-President, the Leader of the Senate and the Leader of the House of

Representatives. Our job is any investigative or security procedure that has sufficient importance to need to transcend the dividing lines all the other organisations have to heed. We can command their support and where necessary we can overrule."

" That makes you very important people."

" We are." Strangely the words did not sound arrogant. The statement had been matter of fact and Adams raised Comoy several notches in his already high esteem.

"I take it you're here in England simply for the Conference?"

" Yes. Our man here is Frank Hunt. It was felt that the nature of the meeting, the important and necessarily complex security operation needed someone with overall command. Colonel Hunt is an experienced man, but not sufficiently experienced in this type of thing. So they sent me."

" And the mysterious man in the Surrey motel?" Comoy rested his forearms on his knees and stared at the Commissioner. His dark features were still expressionless but there was in his eyes something the Commissioner could not quite define.

" That was right out of the blue Commissioner. Totally unexpected. And very worrying. Particularly now he has killed the girl. If that hadn't happened I would probably still be taking a chance and not telling you, hoping I was wrong. As I said, it's a complicated business and I'll start at the beginning. The unit I work for is new, it's been in operation for five years. Before that I was with the F.B.I. I was one of dozens who were drafted into Dallas in November 1963." Adams sat up straight and Comoy fixed him with his dark eyes.

" Yes. The assassination of President Kennedy. You will know enough to know that the police procedures followed there left a great deal to be desired. What you don't know is that after the first few days of chaos some of the police work

66

that took place was quite remarkable. The part that concerns us now is a fingerprinting exercise that took place in the Texas School Book Depository at the corner of Houston and Elms.

"You know that it was established beyond reasonable doubt that all the shots came from there. You can forget the second gunman on the overpass theory. When the F.B.I. moved in the building was sealed off and it was decided to dust the entire building. Every inch. Floors, walls, ceilings, windows, doors, pipes, radiators, tables, chairs, desks, packing cases, the roof, outside walls, the basement, everything. Everything. Even the neon sign on the roof.

"The task was, well I don't have to tell you, the task was a big one. And the results when we looked at them were staggering. Obviously a large part of the building produced nothing. Most of the rest was covered in smears and again we lifted nothing. Where there were prints there were overlaps and partials and, well as I said, it was a big job. When we had finished we catalogued what we'd got together with a note of where they were lifted.

"Then we fingerprinted everyone who had been in the building, or on it, in the two weeks up to November twenty-second and in the days after until we sealed it off. Everyone we could find that is. Employees, customers, delivery drivers, the floor-laying crew who were working there at the time, police, newspaper reporters, t.v. men, our own men.

"Then we started elimination procedures. When we had finished that we were down to about fifteen per cent of the original number of prints. That was when we started on people who had used the building months and even years before. It wasn't a new building you know. It had had a lot of occupiers in the past. You know that depending upon the atmospheric conditions a print can last for a long time. We found prints going back almost two years. And we traced almost everyone of them.

"When that was done we were down to seventeen un-accounted sets. From their location and their age we eliminated twelve from the list. The remaining five included one set from the basement, two sets from the first floor, the ground floor to you, and two from the stairway on the north-west corner. All those five were made, we reckoned, within three months of the date of the shooting. Three were left handed and two were right. It was faintly possible that the left and right hands could have been paired so we had between three and five prints we were interested in.

"Those five prints were sent to every known fingerprint department of every police and military organisation in the world with whom we had that kind of relationship. We did not tell any of them where the prints were from. The print your Inspector Walters found on the menu card at the motel in Surrey matched one of the two sets of prints that were taken from the first floor of the building. That man, the man who stayed at the motel and then disappeared was in the Texas School Book Depository in Dallas, Texas at some time between September first and two days after President Kennedy was assassinated." Comoy stopped speaking and in the silence that followed Adams was conscious of a feeling he had not experienced for years, a surging excitement.

"Of course there's a hell of a lot of assuming going on," Comoy was speaking again, "that is the only fact we have, that he was there and that he was at the motel. We don't know that he was involved with the shooting, we don't know he killed the waitress to stop her giving his description to the Surrey police. We don't know that he is here in England because the President is coming here next week. We don't know any of that. But I do know that in the circumstances we cannot take any risks. No risks at all. Until someone shows me cast iron proof to the contrary I have to assume that an assassination attempt is to be made during the conference. And I have to assume that the likely target is David

Leeson, President of the United States of America."

*　　　*　　　*

The three men sat in silence each reading a copy of the report. The old man finished first and sat staring out of the window. The stocky man looked at the old man's profile with an expression of defiance on his face. It was the young man who, for once, spoke first.

" You should not have asked for this report."

" I have the authority to make the request."

" You were specifically instructed not to make it."

" That is not the point. You know the importance of the situation in London, I felt we had to be certain, the entire operation could have been jeopardised."

" Perhaps, that is not the point. The situation is not only important it is also extremely delicate. This kind of stupid action can . . ."

" Oh for God's sake."

" Stop it." The old man's papery voice cut in. " It is done, there is no point in pursuing the discussion." He glanced at the stocky man, his eyes piercing. " Is there anything else? Any other actions you have taken without our knowledge that have a bearing, direct or indirect, upon this operation?"

The stocky man looked from one to the other of his two companions and for the first time he looked uncomfortable and beneath the defiance there were slight signs of fear.

" Yes."

" What?"

" I sent instructions to Perring, weeks ago now, I ordered him to get closer to Mrs. Ainsley."

" What do you mean, get closer?" The old man's voice was very quiet.

" He has a reputation with women. I told him to exploit his . . . his expertise and seduce her."

69

" My God." The young man stared at the speaker in disbelief. " You told him to do that? With the wife of the British Foreign Secretary? You must be mad."

" Why? It could have been useful, the extra information he may pick up and the possibility of using his power over her for other purposes."

" What extra information? She is the man's wife not his secretary. She won't know anything we don't have already and as for power. What power? Power to blackmail? What use would that be?" The stocky man did not answer and in the silence that fell only the old man's hoarse breathing could be heard. After a moment he turned to the young man.

" Have we time to replace Perring?"

" No. We either proceed as planned or we abort."

" We do not abort. We have to proceed. Too much is at stake and the timing is right and the circumstances may never be repeated. What precautionary measures can we take?"

" Not many, if any at all. Perring is the only one who can get Stellman the equipment he needs. At least in the time available. We could tell Perring to pull out of his entanglement but it might confuse or even frighten him. He is not the most reliable of men but his part is small. No I think we have to take a chance. We have to chance that Perring's experience with women is sufficient to ensure that her husband does not find out before the job is done."

" And afterwards?"

" Afterwards there will be no problems, no problems at all."

" Good." The old man turned to gazing out of the window once more. After a moment the others gathered their papers together and rose to leave the room. The old man looked up at the one spoken of as his successor. A silent message passed between them. A change was about to take place in the heirarchy of the organisation.

70

* * *

In London the Sleeper sat by the window of his bedroom. The seat had become a refuge for him during the weeks that had passed since the thirtieth anniversary message had arrived. He slept badly. He had little stomach for work too but it was there and could not be delegated and it did serve to occupy his mind and give him respite from the mental agony of the task he had been set by those three men far away. He had known for years that if he was called it would be in connection with something big but he had never dreamed it would be the kind of thing they had given him to do. When he had thought about it he had assumed that a task employing his wide and expert knowledge would be placed before him. Not anything as crudely basic as the one he worried over every night as he sat in the chair by the window overlooking the London garden. But there was nothing that he could do to change things. Their orders were explicit and they had to be obeyed.

* * *

But there was another thing that troubled him. Just as he was angry that his first orders for thirty years had been what they were so he knew, with thoughts that were slowly surfacing from his subconscious, that what he had feared would happen to him as the years passed and he became so deeply involved in his artificial life in England had already happened.

71

FOUR

The two women in the yellow Triumph Dolomite had not spoken since starting their journey. That was not unusual. The young one, pretty in a sulkily dumpy way, stared ahead as if hypnotised by the rhythmic movement of the windscreen wipers. The man in the rear seat kept clenching and unclenching his fingers as the car jerked and swung erratically along the road. The older woman was driving badly. Her concentration was poor and she spent more time glancing sideways at the fixed profile of her companion than she did at the road unfolding in front of the car. She made up her mind to have a real talk that evening. She had to find out what it was that was troubling . . . The small van ahead of them moved out suddenly without indication and the movement registered only on the peripheral vision of the driver of the Triumph. Without thought she reacted to the new situation and her reaction was to swing the wheel wildly to the right. The yellow car was suddenly on the wrong side of the road. The driver of the container lorry coming in the opposite direction jabbed a toe at the brake pedal and in an instant felt his heavy vehicle begin to jack-knife on the slick road. He instinctively lifted his foot and the massive silver painted truck lurched forward as it tried to regain its momentarily impaired momentum. The yellow car was caught by only the merest edge of the offside wing of the lorry but it was enough. The car was thrown inwards to crash against the side of the small van and then thrown back again to go under the oncoming rear wheels of the lorry still moving slightly crabwise from that first tentative attempt at braking.

Strangely enough none of the five people involved in the accident heard the shattering crashing noises as the smart yellow car was turned in immeasurable seconds into a twisted parody of what it had once been.

*   *   *

The meeting between the Home Secretary and the Metropolitan Police Commissioner was being held at Scotland Yard at the request of the Minister. He had decided that the change of office scene would be better for him. He was not certain how he had arrived at that assumption but he did not argue with the thought. A few hours away from the familiar four walls was a relief. And for a change the meeting was going well. Peter Evans had never really understood his feelings towards the Commissioner. He had the highest possible regard for a man who was one of the top three or four policemen in the country and who was undoubtedly one of the more imaginative incumbents of that particular office there had been for a long time. But there was always a tenseness. Had he thought about it Evans would have found a number of possible reasons for the unease he always felt but he did not think about it.

Instead he accepted that he would never relax with the man anymore than he would ever relax with most of the men he met in his professional life.

His rise in the political arena had been rapid but not as a result of any genius or specific gift. He had always been noted for his ability to work hard and selflessly at any task he was given. Had he taken up any other profession he would still have reached the top or at least to very near the top. He could never do a job badly or even half-heartedly. Whether he enjoyed the work he was set, or even approved of it, was completely irrelevant.

73

When he applied to become a candidate at a by-election brought about by the death of the member for a small East Anglian town his total commitment to any task had proved to be his greatest weapon. As a result he was chosen as candidate for the marginal seat, despite the greater experience of other contenders for the party's support, simply through having assimilated, over many sleepless nights, every scrap of information he could find about the constituency. This had impressed the committee who were tired of strangers using them and their votes to get to Westminster without caring about the people who put them there.

Once selected as candidate Evans had worked even harder during the campaign that followed. His energy surprised everyone, even the campaign manager who thought he had seen everything. He had never seen anyone like Peter Evans. In the course of the campaign Evans did the impossible, he spoke personally to at least one member of every household in the constituency and again his newly acquired knowledge of local affairs worked a minor miracle. He went into the campaign trying, against the national trend, to hold on to the former member's slender majority. He did so with staggering success, so much so that Charles Fox brought him straight into the Opposition's front benches and exploited the victory to sway public opinion his way. At the next general election the party won well and Fox did not forget the efforts of Peter Evans. He started with a junior post but his inability to do anything by halves soon made him outstrip the constraints of the unimportant job. Fox gave him the Home Office in the same re-shuffle that had brought Ainsley to the Foreign Office. Evans was delighted and he flung himself with his customary enthusiasm into the enormously heavy work load.

*　　*　　*

That was when Peter Evans discovered his flaw. His enthusiasm and energy were uncontrollable. He could not help working hard, the harder the job the harder he worked. So long as he had been in posts with an attainable end he revelled in reaching that end with the greatest possible despatch. But the job at the Home Office was very different. However hard he worked he never began to break the back of the accumulated work-load.

He worked harder and harder and slept less and less. His wife began to turn from him and then his daughter and gradually he found there was no one, no one to whom he could turn for help. And he needed help. He was like a man set the task of counting the grains of sand on the shore knowing that he could never do it and knowing that if he stopped trying he would drown. He lost the ability to relax or to laugh but his natural introspection left his exterior as it had always been, calm and untroubled. No one knew how he really felt.

*　　*　　*

He turned his mind to the problems that had brought him to Adams' office and to Adams himself. He had the feeling that this was a man he should be able to talk to but he knew he never would. With an effort he made himself concentrate on the job before them.

The preparations for the Conference had been hurriedly put together in keeping with the hurriedly assembled agenda for what three months before had been a suddenly presented opportunity for a major Summit meeting. Ideally there were several places in the world more suitable for such an assembly but there had never been any hesitation or doubt that it should be held in London.

The opportunity to play host to the powers of the world was too great to miss. Too great a political advantage to let slip by and Charles Fox was ever an astute politician.

"That leaves the Americans. What is their Embassy proposing?"

"Pretty much the same as the others sir. We have an easier security job with Grosvenor Square. We simply close it off. All persons with a legitimate reason for being in the area immediately prior to the President's arrival and during his stay have been screened and given passes."

"No problems there?"

"Not really. A few affronted citizens complained that they were not to be expected to show passes to go about their lawful business but they were talked round." The Home Secretary nodded.

"The route from there to the Conference Centre?"

"Like the others it's difficult to protect. Very difficult. But we have worked out a variety of routes and there are four men, two British, two Americans who have the authority to order which route is taken each day. They will not consult with each other. They will alternate on a random basis. That way no one is given advance notice."

"Surely that makes surveillance on the route more difficult."

"Only in terms of manpower. We have all routes under permanent observation. Whichever route is taken on any day will be covered."

"You won't be closing off the streets?"

"No sir. With four delegations each moving between its own Embassy and the Conference Centre and our own people, we would end up by closing off half central London."

"It leaves a lot of opportunity for trouble."

"Yes I'm afraid it does but the uncertainty of it all is sufficient to give us just as much advantage as a potential ass . . . troublemakers."

"You were going to say assassin."

"Naturally that's what we're guarding against."

" You haven't any reason to suspect that an attempt is to be made on any of the Heads of State?"

" No sir, no specific reason but obviously that is at the back of all our minds."

" Are you getting full co-operation from all the other security forces?"

" Yes I must say that has been a very unexpected bonus. Everyone has been very good indeed. Everyone."

" I suppose that might be taken as a sign of the likely outcome to the conference. Co-operation."

" Difficult to say sir. We are co-operating because we have to, it's in our mutual interest and we are all here for the same reason."

" And we politicians are not?"

" I didn't say that."

" No Commissioner you didn't, I did. And I'm afraid it's true. Or largely true. You are professionals all working to a common aim and so co-operation is a natural development. We are not professionals. We are amateurs with the fate of nations in our hands and we are not working to a common aim. Oh, we all want peace and prosperity but we all want a little more peace and a little more prosperity for ourselves, for our own nation. That way we find co-operation a word like any other. We make it mean what we want it to mean." The Home Secretary stopped and looked at the Commissioner bleakly for a moment. He saw what he expected to see. A heavily built but graceful man, strong in appearance and manner and not doubt-filled. He wished again that he could confide in the man, relieve himself of some of the doubts that tormented him. Then the moment passed and he closed his mind to the outside.

*   *   *

Adams read the signs on the Home Secretary's face very

accurately. He had seen the same sequence of expressions pass over many faces in the past. Faces of men torn between wanting to confess something and yet prevented from doing so by other intolerable pressures.

He wondered about the man. Since his appointment as Commissioner he had worked under only one other Home Secretary. He had not got on very well with the other one either. But for different reasons. The Minister with the previous government had been a man with fixed views on almost every aspect of his job. Fixed, right or wrong and Adams had felt that mostly he had been wrong. A strong Home Secretary was one thing, a man with prejudices so deeply rooted as to no longer appear to be prejudices was far less acceptable.

Peter Evans was not flawed in the same way. He was weak where his predecessor had been strong, he doubted where the other man had never questioned and he was close where the other had been open.

The Commissioner looked at the face before him. It was weakly handsome. As a young man he had probably been good-looking but the years had not added authority, instead they had only highlighted the inadequacies.

" You had the note about seeing the Prime Minister?" Adams came out of his reverie.

" Yes I have, thank you. I'm seeing him tomorrow."

" Yes, he just wants a word about the arrangements, about all the effort that has gone into the security operation." Evans stood up abruptly. " I'd better get back." At that moment the telephone rang and Adams answered it.

" Yes?" He listened and then looked up at the Home Secretary, he motioned with his hand and in response Evans sat down again. After a moment Adams spoke again, " Thank you." He replaced the instrument carefully and looked at the Minister. " I'm afraid I have some bad news for you. The Hampshire police have reported a road accident. Your wife's car was involved." Evans stood up again.

" Linda," he said.

" They are at the District hospital at Basingstoke. I'll arrange for you to be taken straight there."

" Yes, thank you. Good God. What . . . did they say how badly?"

" No they didn't but I gather it is serious. There were three people in the car. They are all at the hospital."

" Yes, my wife and my daughter were together and there would be the security man with them."

" Shall I call your office."

" Yes please tell them . . . tell them . . ."

" I'll explain what has happened. If you go down a car will be waiting." Adams watched Evans leave the room and for the first time since he had known him he felt a twinge of fellow feeling for the man. He reached for the telephone and made arrangements for a car. When he had done that he told the operator to get the Hampshire force back on the line. He spoke that time to the Chief Constable and he made certain requests that probably seemed unnecessary to the other man but which were agreed to without exception and without question.

*　　*　　*

When the telephone rang in the office Harry Walters shared he answered it only to get a moment's respite from the accumulated paperwork covering the motel robberies. The axe had still not fallen and he found concentration difficult. The call was for him and the message was totally unexpected.

" Walters. This is Macrae. Drop whatever you're doing and go over to Basingstoke. You have an appointment in an hour's time at the central station with the Hampshire Chief Constable and don't ask me why because I don't damned well know. Right?"

" Yes sir."

" Right." The telephone was banged down at the other end of the line by an obviously angry Superintendent. Walters did not need second telling. Any break away from what he had been doing was welcome and in any event there was no time for sitting thinking. Basingstoke was far enough away to need every minute of the hour he had available. As it was he arrived before the Chief Constable and was unable to satisfy any of the unspoken queries from the Basingstoke personnel who were also in the dark over the Chief Constable's impending visit. When the head of the County arrived he swept into the station looking totally unlike any other policeman Walters had ever seen. The uniform he wore was the only thing about him that spelled policeman and even that looked out of place on the tall angular figure. He had commandered an office and was sitting opposite to Walters waiting for the ordered tea to arrive within seconds of his arrival. He stared down his thin nose at the Inspector and when he spoke the voice sounded faintly accusatory but not at all unfriendly.

" You seem to have friends in high places?"

" Sir?"

" Commissioner Adams at the Met. Asked for you to be brought up here. From what they tell me down in Surrey they're damn glad to be rid of you. What did you do? Rape the Chief Constable's wife? Eh?" The noise that followed startled Walters until he realised it was a laugh. He probably looked as bewildered as he felt and the high-ranking officer took pity on him. " Well you seem to know as much about it as I do. Seems there is an investigation taking place here that the Met. is interested in. They want you to see if you can tie it in to whatever it is you're working on?"

" The motel robberies?"

" Eh. No. A murder enquiry. Some girl down at Hindhead."

" That?"

" So they say. Look all this is happening too quickly for me and it seems for you too. We'd better talk to Adams." The Chief Constable reached for the telephone and issued instructions. Then he sat and stared at Walters until the Inspector began to feel even more uncomfortable. The ring ing of the telephone came as a relief.

" Adams. Ratcliffe here. Got that man you wanted here too. Walters. Seems he knows as little as I do. You'd better talk to him." He handed the instrument across the desk to Walters who took it feeling that it was time he woke up.

" Walters speaking sir."

" Inspector. Sorry this was sprung on you without prior explanation but we had to move quickly. There has been a traffic accident not far from where you are sitting now. One of the vehicles involved was a car carrying the wife and daughter of the Home Secretary. The crash is being inves-tigated for any sign of outside influences. I want you to work with the officer in charge. Yours is a watching brief only. You are watching for any connection with the man from the motel. Your mental picture of him is as good as anything we have. After all you're the one the girl, the waitress, gave it to. Any suspicion that he might have been involved report straight back to me. Direct, understand? Not through chan-nels."

" Yes sir."

" Good. They will put you into contact with the enquiry team. And Walters. The girl's murder. Don't blame yourself about that. There was no reason for you to expect that to happen, no reason at all. No one else in your position would have placed her under guard so don't let it prey on your mind."

" Thank you sir."

" Put the Chief Constable back on will you?" Still feeling as if he was dreaming the Inspector handed back the telephone and waited as the Chief Constable made one or two monosyllabic replies to the man at the other end of the line.

*　　*　　*

It was clear from the activity surrounding the wrecked yellow Triumph that Walters could not advance the enquiry there. He asked to be kept notified and headed for the scene of the accident. There too he decided against spending any time. The accident had happened on a stretch of the A30 that passed through open country and from the description of the weather at the time he felt certain that the chances of any casual observers being around were slim. He went back to Basingstoke and after asking for copies of the statements of the drivers of the other vehicles involved he went to the hospital.

The doctor he saw gave him the kind of impatient co-operation he had grown accustomed to over the years.

"No you cannot see any of them at the moment. The woman and the man are both critical. They're unconscious and likely to stay that way. Their chances are slim to say the least. The girl is not so badly hurt. But she also is unconscious. She keeps talking but it's delirious and meaningless, not that we're taking notes."

"Can I take notes?"

"What. You mean sit there and take it down?"

"Yes."

"No. You'd be in the way."

"What about a tape recorder? Can I rig one in the room? With a microphone somewhere so it will pick up what she says."

"Well I suppose it's possible. What's all the fuss about? Isn't it just another road accident?"

"Yes it is as far as we know but you know who they are don't you?"

" Yes. Okay, I can see you have to check these things. Do that if you think it will help. I'll tell the Sister you're doing it. She'll tell you where you can put your recorder and your microphone." The doctor grinned suddenly at the thought his last words brought to mind and he went off looking more cheerful than he had at any time during his talk with the Inspector. Walters went down the corridor in search of a public telephone. The co-operation he received from the station showed that the Chief Constable had left no one in any doubt about the importance of what he was doing.

*   *   *

He wandered back towards the wards where the two female victims were, checking faces automatically as he did so. He recognised the Home Secretary, his face looking paler and more drawn than it had on any of the occasions he had seen it on television or in newspaper photographs. The Minister was talking to the doctor Walters had spoken to earlier and the Inspector kept away as he had a sudden thought that his instructions had not been explicit on one point. He went back to the telephone and called Scotland Yard. He was through to the Commissioner with commendable speed.

" Yes Walters?"

" Nothing to report sir, just a query. The Home Secretary is here, sir. Do you want me to tell him what I'm doing?" There was a long silence at the other end of the line and Walters had the uneasy feeling he had stumbled into a dark corner. After a moment the Commissioner answered.

" I think the Minister has enough on his mind at the moment Inspector."

" Yes sir, I understand." Walters stood staring at the wall for several long moments after he had replaced the receiver until a man tapped him on the shoulder and he stepped aside to let him use the telephone.

* * *

He waited near the entrance to the hospital until the car
arrived. The recorder was small, compact and the microphone looked the part for what he wanted. He went down
the corridor again and found the Sister. He told her who he
was and she agreed to help with the same air of resigned co-
operation the doctor had shown.

" Where is Mr. Evans at the moment?"

" He has gone down to the admin. office. He has several
telephone calls he has to make and it wasn't really con-
venient to make them from here."

" Good."

" Why?"

" Why what?"

" You said good. Why is it good that he is out of the
way?"

Walters thought fast.

" He has enough to worry about at the moment," he said,
unconsciously repeating the Commissioner's comment, " I
don't want him thinking there is anything more to worry
about."

" And is there? Anything more to worry about?"

" Probably not but we need to know all we can about the
accident. The wife and the security man can't help so that
leaves the girl."

The Sister was satisfied at last and she took him into the
room where the girl lay and he arranged the recorder behind
the bedside table and secured the microphone to the leg of
the table with adhesive tape. When he was finished the
whole arrangement was relatively unobtrusive. Not that he
had attempted to hide it completely from sight. That was
not part of his instructions. He switched on and left the
machine running silently on its batteries. He checked his

watch and made a mental note to go back to change the cassette over when it would be nearing the end of its running time. That done he went in search of a cup of tea.

He found one in the staff canteen and he also found the ward sister he had spoken to in Linda Evans' room. He walked over and smiled.

"Taken?" He pointed at the empty chair at the same table. The sister glanced round the room. About five of the forty or so tables were occupied. She smiled up at the policeman.

"No." Walters sat down and felt suddenly slightly ill at ease. He had not been completely celibate since his divorce but any relationships that had happened had been with women fairly low down on his personal scale of reckoning. The choice had been deliberate. He didn't want an entanglement. The sister was different. Apart from her physical appearance which didn't leave much for any man to complain about she was obviously intelligent and well towards the top of his scale. Christ, he thought, what am I thinking about? All I'm doing is having a cup of tea with someone I probably won't see again after this week. Some of his thought processes must have been close to the surface.

"You look worried. Is it the job or just life in general?" Walters shook his head.

"Neither, or maybe both."

"My word, perhaps I shouldn't have asked."

"Sorry." Walters looked at her and grinned. "I really am sorry. I get like this occasionally, you know the kind of thing, is it all worth while?"

"I know."

"Yes, you would, there are a lot of similarities aren't there? Your job and mine. The messy end of life, other people's problems and at the end of it all no real hope that anything will ever change."

"You don't believe that."

85

" Don't I?"

" At this moment perhaps but not the rest of the time."

" Maybe not but moments like this seem to get closer together these days, I'm afraid that one day I will wake up to find that I feel this way all the time, the moments have all run together into one."

" I know the feeling but I think you're wrong."

" I hope you're right."

" Has your little recorder picked up anything? Or shouldn't I ask?"

" No it hasn't and no you shouldn't."

" Sorry." The sister pushed back her chair and stood up.

" Don't go, I wasn't being officious."

" I know you weren't. I have to go, I work here you know."

" Yes. When are you off duty?"

" Why?"

" Why? Well I thought . . . I was going to ask . . ."

" Start by asking my name."

" What? Oh Christ, I'm sorry."

" Don't be and it's Helen. Helen Morrison."

" Helen."

" Yes and what were you going to ask me?"

" What you did with your off duty time but then I don't get all that much of that myself."

" If I have untangled all that correctly are you asking me for a date?"

" Yes."

" Then I accept but heaven knows when it will be."

" That's okay, this is a special job I'm here on anyway. I expect things will ease up in a couple of weeks. When it does I shall have some leave days due. Maybe I can take them to coincide with your days off."

" That would be nice."

" Yes I think it will be. By the way my . . ."

". . . name is Harry Walters," she finished for him. " I've already found that out for myself." She turned to go and halfway to the door she stopped and looked back at him. " In answer to the question you will probably think of in five minutes from now, no I am not married. I was but that's part of the hazards of this job."

" Welcome to the club."

" I had guessed as much. Maybe we will have something in common after all, unlikely though that might seem." She grinned suddenly and was gone before he had time to reply.

*　　*　　*

He sat at the table for another ten minutes thinking. He had always had a carefully protected streak of cynicism but for once he ignored it. He didn't believe in love at first sight and he didn't really think he would ever again want to marry but nevertheless there was something about Helen Morrison that had struck a response in him he had not felt since the early days with his ex-wife. He found himself looking forward to the present job ending and at the prospect of taking his long overdue leave days. That alone was significant, it was the first time for months that he had wanted to have time off work.

*　　*　　*

Saturday mornings had ceased to have any special significance for Adams many years before. Apart from his annual holiday and one long weekend he had not had an entire Saturday off for over a year. That morning he sat at his desk reading the reports from the Basingstoke police as he had a little time before his appointment at Downing Street. The telephone rang and he answered it without taking his eyes off the papers before him.

" Yes."

" Inspector Walters is here sir, asking to see you urgently."

" Walters here? Send him up." Adams frowned slightly as he replaced the receiver. He looked again at the summary on the accident report before him and thoughtfully pursed his lips.

*　　*　　*

Walters was trying hard not to be awed and with only slight success. He had been to the Yard on a number of previous occasions but those had been organised educational visits and he was not accustomed to the treatment he was getting that day. The sudden unexpected association with Chief Constables and American Embassy staff and now with the Metropolitan Police Commissioner was proving too much. He was aware that in terms of rank the Commissioner was only on a par with the Chief Constable he worked for and the one he had been with the previous day at Basingstoke but in terms of public esteem there was no doubt the Commissioner held the top job. And for a few moments Harry Walters felt as out of place as a member of the public and was subject to the same misplaced thoughts. He was shown into the Commissioner's office and stood uncertainly for a moment.

" We meet at last Inspector." The Commissioner pointed to a chair. " Sit down."

" Thank you sir."

" I wasn't expecting you Inspector."

" No sir. I'm sorry I should have telephoned you first."

" No I wasn't rebuking you, Inspector. I assume the reason you're here is a good one."

" Yes sir I'm afraid it is."

" You're afraid it is?

" Yes sir."

" Perhaps you'd better tell me what you have found."

Adams sat back and looked at Walters. There was an air about the younger man that resembled himself when young and that more than anything made the Commissioner think that whatever the Inspector had found out was not going to be a waste of time.

" First of all sir, I have found nothing to tie in the man from the motel." Walters looked at the report still open on the Commissioner's desk. Adams glanced down at it.

" Yes I have seen the report. You know the gist of it Inspector?"

" Yes sir. No suspicion of foul play. A straightforward accident."

" That's right. And you've found nothing that makes you think otherwise?"

" Correct sir. It's . . . It isn't very easy to say sir. At the hospital yesterday the doctors were quite clear that I could have no contact with either Mrs. Evans or the security officer. You know he died in the night do you sir?"

" Yes I do. And I'm afraid the news about Mrs. Evans isn't too good either."

" Yes I know sir. Well the doctor said that the young girl, Linda Evans, was delirious but not as ill as the others. He wouldn't let me stay with her but he did agree to let me put a tape recorder beside her bed in case anything she said might have helped. You must remember sir that at the time the investigation of the crash was not complete and I was still regarding the matter as a possible attempt on the lives . . ."

" That's alright Inspector, don't excuse what you did. It seems to have been a good idea in the circumstances. A little unorthodox perhaps but that doesn't make it any less good. I take it your recorder picked up something that affects the case?" Walters looked suddenly very uncomfortable and the Commissioner knew that the Inspector was battling with a difficult decision.

"Not exactly sir, in fact not at all. The recorder picked up quite a lot of Miss Evans' voice and most of it was meaningless. Just delirious talk as the doctor had said. But some of it made sense. It also picked up the voice of the Home Secretary."

Walters looked at the Commissioner and Adams saw that they had reached the matter that was troubling the Inspector.

"I see. Go on."

"Following our telephone conversation I didn't tell Mr. Evans what I was doing there. He didn't know the recorder was playing. He talked to his daughter quite freely although most of the time she doesn't seem to have been aware of his presence." Walters stopped again and took a deep breath before continuing. "The parts of the girl's talking that wasn't incomprehensible included some statements about her father, those and the statements made by Mr. Evans are . . . well sir I think you should read them. I've brought a transcript. I've also brought the cassettes so that you can listen yourself. I . . . I typed the transcript myself sir. So far no one else knows what is on them."

"I see. Let me see the transcript." Adams reached out a hand and the Inspector pulled a thin folder from his briefcase and handed it to the older man. Adams opened the folder and began to read. In the silence that followed Walters found himself concentrating on distant sounds. The sounds were muffled by the insulation but they were enough to make him pleased he worked in a country area albeit a densely populated one. He was listening to the fading sound of a jet heading into Heathrow when the Commissioner finished reading the notes and laid them back into the folder. He closed the folder with deliberate care and looked at his hands for some time before looking up at Walters.

"You were right to act as you did Inspector. Right to bring the information straight to me and right to ensure no one else had access to either the recordings or the transcript.

You have the recordings with you, you said."

" Yes sir." Walters took the cassettes from the briefcase. " There are quite a few sir. As you'll appreciate a lot of them are just blank, when the girl was sleeping."

" Yes. I understand. I will give you a receipt for these. No. The formalities have to be observed. You must have proof of your action in handing them to me." Adams pulled a pad towards him and wrote for a moment, before tearing off the sheet and handing it to the Inspector. " Thank you. Now. You are to remain on detachment. You remember Mr. Comoy? He has asked that you work with him. For the same reason I asked you to go to Basingstoke. You are the nearest thing we have to an eyewitness. He is trying to find our mystery man and you will work with him. Two points. First Mr. Comoy is a very senior official, do as he requests and do not report your actions to anyone. Second do not mention this," he gestured at the folder and the pile of cassettes he had laid neatly upon it, " to anyone, anyone at all without permission, personally given permission from me."

" I understand sir. Where do I find Mr. Comoy?"

" At the American Embassy. He isn't expecting you yet. I had planned to talk to you later today. I suggest you telephone him from downstairs. If he isn't available talk to Colonel Hunt."

" Yes sir." Walters stood up clutching his briefcase. He hesitated an instant as the Commissioner held out a hand. The two men shook hands and Walters left the office simultaneously relieved to be rid of the burden he had brought to the Commissioner and bewildered at the new turn in events that was sending him to the American Embassy.

*　　*　　*

Behind him the Commissioner sat staring at the wall before

pressing a button on his intercom. He ordered his car to be ready in five minutes. Then he locked the folder and the cassettes into his desk drawer. That done he stood up and straightened his uniform jacket. He picked up his cane and gloves and hat as he left the office. Quite suddenly he was no longer looking forward to the meeting with the Prime Minister.

*   *   *

Downing Street had the customary smattering of foreign tourists taking photographs of the front door of Number Ten and the attendant policemen. There was a sudden scurry as they all focussed on the Commissioner's car as it arrived. Probably none of them knew who he was but it was some activity to record on their films for their friends at home. The Commissioner acknowledged the salutes of the two uniformed constables and for once he forgot his personal rule of at least smiling if not actually speaking to any beat constable with whom he came into contact. The door swung open in the customary fashion before he had reached it and he was able to walk in without breaking step.

*   *   *

He had met Charles Fox on several previous occasions. All but one before he had become Prime Minister. The one occasion since then had been on neutral ground at the Lord Mayor's Banquet. This was the first time he had been to Number Ten and he might have felt a natural awe at being there had it not been for his pre-occupation with Inspector Walters' visit. He was shown upstairs to the Prime Minister's study. The two men shook hands as they greeted one another.

" Please sit down Commissioner. Cigarette?"

92

" Thank you sir." Adams took a cigarette from the proffered box and lit it from the lighter the Prime Minister held for him. Fox picked up the cigarette he had laid on the side of the ashtray when Adams had been shown in.

" I'm pleased we had this opportunity to meet. You possibly do not know it but I was not entirely convinced when it was suggested that the security operation for the Conference should be placed under your control. It was one of the Home Secretary's ideas you know. He has a very high regard for you." He flicked his eyes away from the Commissioner as he saw an expression appear, an expression that showed he had disturbed the normally phlegmatic policeman. He ran over in his mind the words he had spoken since the Commissioner had walked in but found nothing there to account for the unrest.

" That is very kind of Mr. Evans." The Commissioner made the sentence sound like anything other than an expression of pleasure.

" Yes, it seems everything is going well. Very well. All problems safely overcome?"

" All we know about sir." The Commissioner appeared to have recovered from whatever it had been that troubled him.

" Should I read anything into that remark Commissioner?" For an instant Adams regretted the undertaking he had given Comoy, then he set the thought aside.

" No sir, but we are trying to avoid becoming complacent. To do that we have to assume something is going to happen."

" Yes I see what you mean. Everyone has to be alert to any eventuality."

" Yes sir."

" Is there anything I can do?"

" No I don't think so sir. Everything is as controlled as we can make it. The Conference is being approached in a friendly state of mind, if it stays that way then our job

93

will be that much easier."

"Ah well perhaps I can help after all. I will do my best to ensure no one falls out with anyone else."

"Thank you sir." Adams smiled slightly. He sat a little straighter in his chair and the Prime Minister looked at him curiously. "There is another matter sir. Not investigated yet but I think you should know about it at once."

"Yes Commissioner. What is it?" Adams took a deep breath.

"Following the accident to Mrs. Evans and her daughter I had a check made to ensure there was no question of foul play. One of the team working on the enquiry decided to record the delirious words of Miss Evans. The idea was a good one. She might have seen or known something of the last few minutes before the crash."

"And did she?"

"No sir. In any event we are certain now that the crash was purely accidental. But before that was established the girl's words had been recorded at length together with quite a lot of things her father said to her."

"The Home Secretary? You mean this officer recorded a private conversation between the Home Secretary and his daughter?"

"Yes sir."

"Commissioner I'm not sure I like the way this is leading. Are you sure this is a proper matter?"

"I'm very sorry Prime Minister but I have no alternative."

"Very well. Go on."

"The relevant parts of the recordings were transcribed personally by the officer concerned. He was most discreet, no one apart from he and I know of their content. I have yet to listen to the recordings myself, the officer did not get his report to me until a few minutes ago. In addition to not hearing the tapes myself needless to say I have not yet had the opportunity of investigating what appears on the tran-

94

script."

" Well?"

" There seems very little doubt that Mr. Evans is cracking up. Not just tired, I expect most of your Ministers are that. This is much worse. He seems to be, well I'm far from being a medical man and obviously there will have to be investigations by doctors, he seems to me to be in a very strange mental state."

" A strange mental state? What exactly do you mean Mr. Adams?"

" I think he is having a nervous breakdown. It sounds to me as if he is trying to do things in his work that part of his brain is trying to tell him is impossible. At the very least he would appear to need a long rest, at the worst . . . but as I said, sir, there is a need for expert medical examination."

"I see." The Prime Minister was silent for a moment. " This has to be kept very . . . well, I don't have to tell you what to do with regard to secrecy."

" No sir, it will have the highest classification."

" Please leave the matter of Mr. Evans' resignation to me Commissioner. As you will understand I cannot ask for it immediately. We have to be certain. I will read the transcripts myself then if I agree with you, as I am sure I shall, I will have them considered by experts and I shall then arrange for Mr. Evans to be examined. That shouldn't prove too difficult. Then I can act. In the meantime secrecy is needed in view of the forthcoming conference. There must not be the slightest whisper that all is not well in my government. You understand Mr. Adams that I do not say that from a party political standpoint or even from a national standpoint. This conference is a great opportunity for the world and I don't want anything to mar its chances of total success."

" I understand sir."

" How soon can you let me have a copy of the transcript?"
" Later today."
" Thank you Commissioner." The Prime Minister stood up
and held out his hand to the taller man.

*   *   *

After Adams had gone Charles Fox sat at his desk for a long
time, thinking. Eventually he opened a folder in front of
him and began to read, making occasional notes as he did so.
Then he lost his concentration and sat brooding until his
wife came to call him for lunch. He hadn't a lot of appetite
for it.

FIVE

Stellman had arranged the meeting with Perring for Friday
of the following week. He knew Perring would need that
length of time to obtain the equipment he had ordered and
to find a suitable third man. Stellman had quite enough to
do to fill the time. On one day he had driven to Fulham and
bought a small motor-cycle from a dealer there. The
machine was bought by many people who like Stellman did
not want to be bogged down in traffic in the city centre. He
arranged for it to be registered in Carter's name and he left
telling the salesman he would collect it a few days later.

*   *   *

Then he began behaving like a tourist. He visited art galleries and museums taking pleasure in the pleasure he felt. Pleasure made greater by the knowledge that he would never visit England again and that his island home could never give him anything remotely resembling the cultural standards of London.

*   *   *

But he did not forget the reason he was there. On most of the days he spent in the capital he contrived to spend some time in the area he had decided was most suitable for his purpose. He was careful. He drove the Cortina twice on well-separated days, and he walked once on a day when a sudden summer rainstorm allowed him to hurry past well covered in a raincoat and hat. The other days he used taxicabs. He felt certain the place would serve, provided he got the co-operation he needed from the Sleeper, co-operation he knew he would get without question.

*   *   *

Since the day he had spoken to Perring at the number the answering service had given him he had called twice more, both times at the flat he knew Perring occupied in Flood Street. Perring had sounded different to the first time they had spoken. He gave Stellman the information he requested concisely and without comment and the tone Stellman had heard in his voice that first time was absent. But still Stellman worried over his contact. He knew there was little Perring could do that would endanger him. Perring did not know what Stellman was there to do although the information he had been asked to provide and the equipment he had to supply made guessing an easy game. Neither did Perring know how to contact Stellman and he had no idea how Stellman proposed carrying out the job and only the sketchiest idea where he planned to do it. But still Stellman worried.

*   *   *

The Friday meeting had been arranged for late evening. There was very little traffic along Park Lane when Stellman swung the Cortina round into Piccadilly. He turned left again into Old Park Lane and saw Perring's small estate car parked ahead of him. He stopped close behind to prevent Perring from reading his registration number and climbed out. He stood beside the estate car for a moment and checked that Perring was looking straight ahead and that the rear-view mirror had been twisted on its stalk so that Perring could not use it to look at Stellman as he sat in the back seat. Stellman opened the door and slid in. He glanced at the floor area behind the rear seat.

" Everything there?" he asked.

" Yes."

" Any problems with any of them?"

" No, all as you ordered."

" Good. What about the man?"

" All arranged. When do you want to see him?"

" I don't. You can arrange things with him. Tell him to meet me in the car park of the Marquis of Granby. It's a pub I passed the other day. On the A3 at a roundabout at the end of the Kingston By-pass."

" I know it. When?"

" I'll tell you later. Now what are the arrangements for the journeys from the Embassy to the conference centre?"

" Generally as I told you on the telephone. There are four routes, five really but two are almost identical except for a small detour at the start, no pre-determined plan exists for the selection of the route on any given day. The decision on which route is used will be made at the last moment by one of four men. Two British, two American. They will be splitting their duties randomly. Only one of the four will travel in the lead car and that will be the last one to come out of the building. It could be any of them. Whichever one it is, when he is in his seat in the lead car he will instruct the driver which route to follow. The other cars will simply follow the leader."

"So if we arrange for one of those four to hang back on the day he will automatically get to select the route?"

"Yes but how can you arrange that?" Stellman did not answer and a cold silence fell. Perring realised he had stepped over an invisible line and hastily went on with his report on the procedure. "Police are on permanent duty on all routes and they will stop traffic as they see the cars approaching and allow turns where they are prohibited and also where necessary allow the cars to go the wrong way in one-way streets. Two of the routes necessitate the cars driving south down South Audley Street. One of those is the one you are interested in. At the bottom of South Audley Street they will turn either left or right. If it's right it is the one you want." There was silence for a moment before Stellman spoke.

"Good. I'll take everything now. The back door is unlocked?"

"Yes."

"When I close the door drive off immediately. Do not look back."

"I understand."

"Good." Stellman climbed out of the back seat and walking round to the back of the estate car he raised the tailgate and lifted out the two cardboard boxes that lay there. He stood them one upon the other on the road and carefully closed the door. The estate car started at once and Perring drove away. Stellman walked the few paces to the Cortina and opened the rear door. He placed the two boxes carefully on the seat and then climbed into the driving seat.

He waited for another two minutes before driving off. He watched his rear-view mirror very carefully for several minutes before he was satisfied Perring had not stayed in the area.

He was wrong. Perring had stayed in the area but not to follow the other man. He had pulled out into Park Lane and had immediately turned onto the forecourt of the Inn On The Park. He drove down into the basement car-park and left his car for the attendant to slot away somewhere. He walked back up the ramp and stood there for a few minutes. He saw a white Cortina drive past and he was fairly certain it was the one Stellman was driving. He went into the hotel and up to the first floor bar. After his third drink he began to feel a little easier. He was also angry. Angry with himself. First and most immediate he was angry at the unreasoning fear he had of the man he had just left. There was no justification for it he knew, the man was not a threat to him but somehow, in the few minutes' telephone conversation he had had and those few minutes in the car talking to the shadowy figure in the back seat, he had felt menaced.

It had to be senseless. The man could not do without Perring, he needed him. He realised that he was letting himself sink into a trough of self-justification. He needed to feel important and not just a tool for others. It was unlike him to feel that way and he was sure it was because of the other thing that angered him. The affair with Janet Ainsley. Not the substance of the affair itself, he could not have enough of her, what angered him was that he had been ordered into the relationship as if he was an animal. A stud to be used when others demanded. That alone should not have bothered him but it demeaned her and that was what hurt.

*   *   *

He stood his glass on the bar counter with slightly more

force than was needed and a woman sitting along the bar from him glanced up. For an instant their eyes met and Perring began to take an interest. At that moment all thoughts of Janet Ainsley went out of his mind. He needed a woman. Not for love or affection or even for conversation. He needed sex.

* * *

Picking up the woman in the bar had been even easier than usual for him. So easy that if he hadn't had the first three drinks so quickly he might have sensed something was wrong. He had several more drinks before he took her back to the Flood Street flat and what happened then came as close to rape as anything he had ever done with a woman. It fell short of it only because the woman did her best to accommodate him in whatever he did or tried to do. That too should have warned him but it didn't. Even a professional would not have stood for the treatment he gave her, certainly not without first having secured payment.

Eventually he was exhausted and fell away from her and was almost immediately asleep. The woman sat up on the bed and looked at him with disgust. Then she walked over to the mirror and looked at herself with the same expression on her face. But she made no attempt to leave. She began to talk softly to Perring and after a few minutes he began to answer. At first the words were an incoherent jumble, then he began to make sense. The woman picked up her handbag and took out a cigarette case. She opened one side and took out a cigarette and lit it. Then she closed the case, pressed one end and opened the other side to the one that held the cigarettes. She pressed a switch and placed the case on the pillow by Perring's head. She watched the tiny spools of the miniature recorder spin as she smoked the cigarette. After a moment she began to ask questions again.

*　　*　　*

When Perring awoke the next morning he had almost for-gotten the woman from the night before and only the linger-ing smell of her perfume reminded him that he had not been alone. He grinned at the recollection and opened the windows to get rid of the smell. He had forgotten about her almost before the smell had cleared from the room.

*　　*　　*

Harry Walters was working in the dark. He had no real idea what he was doing but so far as he could make out neither did anyone else. He was also very tired. He had been working even longer hours than usual since joining the team at the American Embassy. Normally that would not have bothered him but for once it did. The conversation in the hospital canteen had not been far from his thoughts in the days that had passed.

He had not seen Helen Morrison since but they had talked several times on the telephone. Inadequate conversations, full of rambling stories of episodes in his career but pleasant, easy conversations. He felt slightly self-conscious about it all, as if he was letting someone down by acting out of character. But the character he had become was self-made and he was the only person he was letting down.

*　　*　　*

Within very few days he was starting to admit to himself that he was showing definite signs of being in love and love at first sight too. He was mildly annoyed that a hard-nosed copper should be capable of something like that. He made himself stop thinking about Helen and brought his mind back to reality. The investigation, if that was what it was, confused him. Whatever it was all about there was no doubt the Americans were worried. That and the instructions he had received from the Commissioner had been enough to make him press on. Not that there was much he had to do. Comoy's instructions had been simple. " All we want you to do Inspector is circulate through our security procedures, you have carte blanche, go where you want with whom you want. You're free to go into any area of the security operation we have set up for the President's visit to the conference.

" All you have to do is look out for anyone who resembles the description the girl gave you. Everyone on the team has that description as well, they're all looking too but I have the feeling that your interpretation of it will be nearer the mark than the rest of us will get. Anyway, right or wrong you're an extra man on the team and that will help." There seemed little doubt that the security of the President was involved and Walters felt sufficiently compensated by his involvement in something that important to worry that no one told him anything else. On the Friday night he had been taken aside by the American colonel.

" The President arrives tomorrow Harry. We'll want you with us when we go to meet him."

" Yes sir. What time are you leaving here?"

" Ten. He's due down at two in the afternoon but we need the extra time to check out the field."

" Heathrow isn't it sir?"

" Er, yes, that's right, Heathrow." Hunt had nodded and left Walters who went to bed. Bed meant sleeping in a large room on the ground floor of the Embassy, a room he shared with seven other men, all members of the security staff. None of them talked very much to one another let alone to him but as they never questioned why he was there no disruption threatened their work together. One thing was

103

quite obvious, none of them knew any more about the importance of the man at the motel than he did himself.

* * *

Hunt had not gone to bed after he had left the English police inspector. He had a meeting to attend. Comoy was waiting in the colonel's office and moments after Hunt had walked in the switchboard operator announced the arrival of Commissioner Adams.

" Commissioner, good to see you. I take it you have had no developments since we saw you last."

" No, none at all." Adams' face gave nothing away. The revelations brought to him by Inspector Walters the previous weekend had sparked off a delicate, highly confidential enquiry. The man in charge of the two-man team had reported back to Adams that there was already sufficient evidence to suggest the cassettes filled at the injured girl's bedside were telling a small but true part of the story. Adams had not enjoyed the further reports he had made to the Prime Minister and by the time the meeting with the Americans came on the eve of the President's arrival he was beginning to feel the strain of the events of the past days.

" Same here," Comoy said, " a total blank. We have seen nothing and heard nothing."

" Mr. Comoy, this may seem unlikely to you but we have to consider that if your man is still here and if he was in Dallas in 1963 it does not automatically follow that he is here to make an attempt on the life of President Leeson."

" I don't think he will be here for a holiday Commissioner."

" Neither do I. If he was involved in Dallas then there is every reason to suspect he is here for a purpose that could be lethal for someone."

" Well?"

" It doesn't have to be Leeson. His target, if he has one,

104

could equally well be one of the other visiting heads of state. Korowski, Peng Lo or Duvivier. Or even our own Prime Minister. Or for that matter any of the Foreign Ministers or other senior delegates."

" No, we can rule out a lot of them. If he's after someone then it will be a top man."

" Yes but why Leeson? It can't be for his views of the man's politics. You can't get much further from Kennedy than Leeson. He is diametrically opposed to the kind of things Kennedy wanted. It seems unlikely to me that someone who could assassinate or be involved in the assassination of a man like Kennedy would also want to see the death of David Leeson."

" Your reasoning is sound Commissioner and don't think we haven't covered the point. But if you pursue that line of reasoning you can similarly rule out Korowski and Peng Lo. That leaves Fox and Duvivier and either of them would be an easier target at a time when London is not crawling with security men. No it has to be Leeson, I'm sure of it."

" Then why here? Why not in the States?"

" I don't know. Unless it has something to do with the conference and there wasn't time to set it up before Leeson left Washington."

Adams shook his head gloomily. Logic told him there had to be a link between Kennedy and Leeson. The three men sat in silence for several minutes before Hunt spoke for the first time.

" I take it you want to brief the other security units Commissioner."

" Yes. I think we have to tell them we have reason to believe a known political assassin is in the country. We have to do that at least."

" They will be alert enough as it is."

" But we cannot take the risk. Suppose you are wrong. Suppose an attempt is made on one of the other Premiers, then if it comes out we knew the man was here and had kept it a secret, a secret between the British and the Americans what would happen? It would set back relations between the nations for years. I don't think that is a risk that can be taken."

"Maybe you're right Mr. Adams." Comoy rubbed his eyes with the back of his hand in a weary gesture. "Very well. The President arrives tomorrow the others on Sunday. I have already made a recommendation to the President he has chosen to ignore. I'll see him immediately after he has settled in at the Embassy and give him the whole story. Dallas, the fingerprint, everything. After that I will arrange a meeting with the other security chiefs before the other delegates arrive. It will be up to them how much they reveal."

"You will tell them about Dallas?"

"No. No one will be told that." Adams nodded reluctantly and Comoy looked at him sharply. "You haven't told your Prime Minister?"

"No I haven't and I can't say I'm very happy about it. I think I'm being derelict."

"I don't think he would see it that way."

"Maybe not. Very well, we'll leave it at that. I agree to let matters rest until President Leeson is here. After you have seen him we'll talk again and decide the action we are to take."

Adams stood up and shook hands with the other men. After he had gone the Americans sat in silence for a while.

"We can't do more than we are doing Lewis."

"Maybe not but I feel like a man sitting in the middle of a minefield waiting for someone to come and get me. Whatever I do or if I do nothing the result will be the same. Sooner or later there'll be a bang." Comoy paused for a moment and then left speculation behind. "You've arranged for the policeman, Inspector Walters, to go out with us tomorrow?"

" Yes."

" Good, it might help. Who knows where Air Force One is coming in?"

" You, me, the President and the pilot. Everyone else thinks it is due in at Heathrow."

" Good, see you in the morning Frank. Goodnight."

" Goodnight Lewis." The colonel sat at his desk for another half hour before going to his bedroom. Like everyone else at the Embassy he slept badly that night.

*   *   *

Stellman had carried the two cardboard boxes openly to his room. Neither was particularly bulky or heavy and any casual observer would have assumed them to be purchases made from local shops. He closed the bedroom door and stood the boxes on the bed. He took off the leather gloves he had been wearing and opened his suitcase. He took out the pair of surgeon's rubber gloves he carried everywhere and pulled them on. He slit open the brown paper strip that secured the flaps with a penknife and opened the boxes. The contents had been carefully wrapped in tissue paper and there were polystyrene fillers to stop the contents moving about. He spread one sheet of tissue on the bed and one by one he lifted the items from their containers and placed them carefully ready for examination.

*   *   *

The first weapon was a new nine millimetre Beretta semi-automatic. Single action, it was a useful gun for the purpose he had in mind. The second weapon was special. He had ordered a Walther PPK nine millimetre semi-automatic from Perring because he needed the superb accuracy that weapon would provide. Like the Beretta it was new. Unlike the

Beretta it was double-action to give him the speed of fire that would be necessary in the limited time he would have at his disposal.

* * *

He continued to empty the cardboard boxes. The two Bond shoulder holsters were not new. He needed the suppleness that only use could bring and again Perring had provided precisely what he wanted. For a moment he felt a slight warmth towards the other man but it was merely the warmth of a craftsman being provided with the right tools. When all the other items were laid on the bed he started work . . .

* * *

He cleaned the Beretta first taking care to keep the Hoppe's No. 9 off the black plastic grips. He used the Parker-Hale wool mop to clean the barrel and then carefully lubricated the weapon. He took his time. There was no need to rush and every need to be certain there would be no problems later.

* * *

He broke open the PPK with a swift upward movement and began to clean it. He took even more care than he had with the Beretta. He used the same wool mop and then ran a spiral nylon filament brush through the barrel to finish. Again he was careful to keep the cleaner and lubricant from the plastic grips.

* * *

When he had finished he reassembled the automatic. He

checked that the trigger guard swung down freely and the slide lifted away from the frame without any sticking. He reached over and picked up the yellow and red box containing its full complement of bullets. He checked each one individually for any outward sign of imperfection. There were none. He wiped them over with tissue and then replaced eleven of the copper jacketed shells nose down in their box. He loaded seven into each magazine and then slid the two weapons into their respective holsters. He wrapped tissue paper around each holstered weapon and then placed them into his suitcase. He gathered the cleaning materials and the spare shells into one of the two cardboard boxes and he folded up the remaining box and added that to the contents of the first box. He pushed the suitcase under the bed and placed the cardboard box beside it. When that was done he lay down on the bed and stared into the single electric light bulb. He lay there for a long time feeling the tension creeping through him. Eventually he stood up and undressed. He turned out the light and opened the curtains.

The room faced east and he stared at the glow in the sky over London and thought about the men who were there in the city. Men he had to outwit. An easy enough matter provided they did not know he was there. He thought about the girl at the motel. It was regrettable he had long decided, regrettable but necessary. He had no choice other than to cover his tracks. Even though there had been a marked possibility that those tracks had been invisible in the first place. He wondered for a moment if any police force anywhere knew of his existence. If they had ever found a fingerprint or a hair or any of the fragments from which they could build so much. He doubted it. He had been very careful in the six jobs he had done in the previous twenty years. Very careful indeed. He had to be to justify the fees he was paid. This was to be the biggest fee yet. And the oddest job. He grinned slightly to himself in the darkness, all thought of the dead girl gone. He was a rich man and he had one asset. Himself. And that asset had to be protected at all costs. That was a simple fact of his economic life. He walked away from the window and climbed into the bed. He closed his eyes and was asleep within seconds.

* * *

In the centre of London one of the men Stellman had been thinking of, one of the men he had to outwit, was thinking about him. Lewis Comoy did not know the name Stellman used, only now, years after he first knew the man existed did he have even the slightest idea what the man looked like. There had been many times during the years that had elapsed since Dallas when Comoy had managed to forget the unknown prints they had lifted from the old building. His work had taken him to many places and into many difficult and dangerous areas of work but always in the moments when he relaxed and thought about the past he came back to them. Those partials. Unknown prints or as the English police called them those unknown marks. Meaningless or meaningful? A mark left by a man who had legitimately entered the building to paint or repair or deliver or collect and who for one reason or another had never been traced. Comoy did not know, yet he had always felt the need for the mark to mean something. Like most Americans particularly those who had worked on the case always at the back of his mind there had been the thought that perhaps, just perhaps, the whole truth had never emerged.

* * *

A remark made by Raymond Adams drifted into his mind. The comment that there was such a wide gulf between Kennedy and Leeson, that the same man would hardly want to kill them both. There was something in that, Comoy silently acknowledged, the unknown man would have to be working for money not for idealism but even so if he was being hired for the job could it be by the same man? Surely not. Equally it could hardly be that the man had been hired by an opposed faction. Unless he was known to two sides as a competent killer and had been hired co-incidentally to kill another President for reasons totally opposed to those that had been behind the original commission.

* * *

Kennedy and Leeson. Two more dissimilar men were hard to imagine. David Leeson had made few friends on his way to the top of the American political tree. Some of his early days had episodes that did not bear close examination but that alone was inadequate ground for Comoy's deep dislike of the man. Other Presidents had similar bad starts to their political careers, Harry Truman for one, and he, while imperfect had proved to be politically stronger and more stable than many had expected.

Leeson represented the same state as had Joe McCarthy and in his early days he had not hesitated to use his notorious predecessor's tactics of slur and half-truthful allegations and when it suited him totally untruthful allegations. Since coming to office he had shown in his handling of foreign policy as much élan as Lyndon Johnson but without the Texan's blundering honesty and in consequence most of the advances made in that field during the Nixon and Ford administrations had vanished.

Close to him he kept advisors who were at least as suspect as those Nixon had gathered about him. His manner, to people close to him, was abrupt to the point of open rudeness and slowly over the four years of the first term that was now drawing to a close he had lost a lot of the support he badly needed. The press had not lost any of the strength it had shown over the Nixon case and against Leeson from the start it was beginning to change public opinion. It had failed to prevent his election in the first place because of the incredible weakness of the opposing candidate. But now people were reading and listening.

*   *   *

One thing was certain, Comoy thought, Leeson would lose November's election and probably by a massive margin. He had kept himself as non-political as a government employee could. He had deliberately refrained from voting for several years, in fact not since Kennedy. He thought back to those days. He had enjoyed the work then, it had seemed valuable, a contribution towards a better world. Second generation Jewish Comoy knew one was needed. Not that his youth had been uncomfortable, his father had seen to it that his only son did not have the same struggle he had experienced. Having only one son had been part of the plan and unusually for parents' plans it had worked. Lewis Comoy had succeeded. First as a lawyer and then in lower echelon politics.

Law enforcement work was something he had never considered and when it was first suggested to him he had laughed at the idea. But the idea had taken root and after the man who had made the original suggestion talked some more it began to sound like a very good idea indeed. Like most Americans his knowledge of the Federal Bureau of Investigation was a mixture of comic strip adventures and a holier-than-thou air. He was intelligent enough not to believe his thoughts and within days of becoming an agent he knew he was in the kind of work he would do for the rest of his life. He had risen rapidly through the ranks and when the government had decided a special department was needed, one separate from and even superior to all existing departments,

112

he had been approached to join. As soon as he learned the far-seeing purpose behind the new operation he had not hesitated to accept the post.

*   *   *

It had brought him closer to the top of American political life than he had ever been before but somehow the early promise faded. He never felt he belonged as much as he had in the early days with the F.B.I. Then, with Kennedy in the White House, he had felt differently. Succeeding Presidents failed to inspire him. And then came Leeson. He had hardly believed the result of the election when it was announced even though he knew the weakness of the opposition. After the election he had toyed with the idea of resigning but he knew he would not. He served an office not a man. As far as possible he avoided close contact with the new President but on the few occasions he was in his presence he knew that the dislike was mutual. And he knew why although at first he hoped he was mistaken.

*   *   *

Anti-semitism was something he had experienced little of and to meet it strongly in, of all people, the President of the United States of America was a terrible shock. But he stayed on, unconsciously growing slightly bitter, but always so much on top of his job that no one could have known how much he despised the man in the White House.

*   *   *

He shook his head wearily, he was getting nowhere. Liking Leeson or not was not an issue, what mattered was that he had to keep him alive and that meant stopping the man who was somewhere off-stage waiting for the right moment. There was no way they could find that man, no way to back-track and find a route to him. All they could do was wait and watch and hope that the security operation was strong enough. Certainly it would be stronger than the loosely flung together protective screen that had covered Dallas fifteen years before. He decided he could do no more that night. He took to bed with him no clues, no leads and no ideas. Just hope. And only faint hope at that.

SIX

As far as duty permitted the Prime Minister had avoided close contact with the Home Secretary. But duty was pressing. The Saturday morning meeting was only the latest of a series of discussions that brought the two men into close contact. The meeting was unavoidable. The first of the foreign Heads of State, David Leeson, President of the United States of America was due to arrive that same afternoon and a snag in the agenda of the first meeting scheduled for Monday morning had arisen.

*   *   *

Peter Evans and Michael Ainsley sat in the Prime Minister's study and the air, already filled with cigarette smoke was becoming strained with the irritations of the matter in hand.

" It's so damned typical. We might have known they would raise the subject."

" Yes Michael, but we didn't know and we should have

done. What are our people in Paris playing at? They should have been onto this weeks ago. Not now. Two days before the talks start."

"Trust the French. Or perhaps it would be better to say never trust the French."

"That is hardly the kind of thing I want to hear my Foreign Secretary say even in private."

"Sorry Prime Minister. But this really is an uncalled for stratagem. The place to air an old grievance about right of access is in private at one of the luncheons or dinners we will be having during next week. That way the Chinese would have found a way to appease Duvivier."

"The Chinese are not noted appeasers."

"Maybe not but they want these meetings to be as successful as possible. The trading benefits they can gain are enormous. I think they would have backed down but now it's public knowledge God knows what they will do. It isn't beyond the limits of possibility they will decide to boycott the conference."

"That must not happen Michael, this is far too important for all of us. Duvivier must be made to see this is a diplomatic blunder."

"Easier said than done. The French still think they invented diplomacy."

"What about the Chinese? Has there been a reaction?"

"Not yet. I've had an informal word with their Ambassador. He seems to think all will be well but he is something of a declared optimist."

"And you Michael are becoming something of a pessimist." Fox lit another cigarette and stared through the smoke at the other men. Evans had not spoken for some time. The subject of the last few minutes' discussion did not directly affect him and he sat looking into space clearly unaware of the words of the others. He looked dejected, understandably enough, and nothing like the man Fox had always thought him to be. Even knowing what the Commissioner had reported to him the Prime Minister still found it hard to believe that Evans was breaking up. There were only the slightest signs of the strain he obviously felt over the accident, nothing more. Fox tried to think of some way to bring him into the conversation, to involve him, fully aware that he should have been at home resting or at the bedsides of his wife and daughter but affairs of the state were not taskmasters that could be lightly set aside. The Prime Minister was relieved that the Home Secretary's part in the conference was small and he was even happier that, correctly, the Minister had delegated to Raymond Adams the entire control of and responsibility for the security operation. He had to be certain that nothing affected the conference plans.

" Peter, any thoughts on the subject?"

" What, er, sorry Charles, I wasn't really listening, were you talking about the security measures?"

" No, but let's talk about that for a moment, there doesn't seem to be much we can do about the French. Now the wheels of diplomacy are moving I suppose we had better keep out from under them. What about the security operation? Any problems? The other day, when I spoke to Mr. Adams everything seemed to be going well."

" Well, yes I suppose so."

" You don't sound very confident. Is there any reason to believe there will be trouble?"

" No, not really, it's just . . . well, I find it hard to believe but I have a feeling there is something going on that I should know about but don't. I heard something the other day, nothing much, just a whisper really but it seemed to suggest the Americans know more than they are saying. There has been a sudden and marked increase in their intelligence activity."

" What has Adams to say about it?"

"Nothing, that puzzles me a little. He dismissed the matter when I raised it, dismissed it as if it was nothing."

"Very probably it is nothing. Adams has a total grasp of the situation and he and the Americans appear to be working well together. Perhaps what you have heard is nothing other than the standard American nervousness where their head of state is concerned."

"Perhaps you're right." Evans nodded slowly and fell back into his reverie.

*　　*　　*

In the silence that followed Ainsley struck a match to light another cigarette and the sudden noise seemed to form a period to the discussion.

"Is there anything else we should talk about now?"

"No I don't think so Charles," Ainsley answered. Evans sat, still silent but he had heard the question that time and shook his head in answer.

"Very well, we'll break off now. We have to prepare to go out to meet the President. We shall travel separately as usual so I will see you both at the airfield."

"Fine, I'll see you later." The Foreign Secretary gathered up his papers. He glanced at Evans who started to rise until the Prime Minister cut in.

"Stay a moment will you Peter, I would like a private word. You go ahead Michael." Ainsley nodded and after a brief curious glance at Evans left the study. Evans sank back into his chair and waited, his face expressionless as ever.

*　　*　　*

Janet Ainsley was walking down Kings Road as her husband was leaving the Prime Minister's study on the first floor at Number Ten Downing Street. She was filled with as much excitement as she had felt the first time she had been with Perring at the house in Kent. Then the magic had been spoiled by the telephone call that had changed Perring. She was completely unaware of the reason for the call, Perring had told her nothing after his first brief reference to his departmental head wanting him. But the call had affected him. They had lain together in the bed but there had been no further love-making. Whatever the call had been about it was strong enough to keep his mind from her. She had resented it at first but the following morning she had seen it in a different light.

He did a difficult job and it was one that could, she knew, be dangerous. He was entitled to be affected by his work. And the memory of the way he had made love to her was enough to make her forgive him almost anything. She also forgave his abrupt decision to travel back to London instead of staying in Kent for the weekend. Since then he had spent his duty hours doing as he always did. Treating her with distant politeness. In his off duty hours he seemed to have disappeared. She had found his address simply enough. She had asked Jennings the man who took the opposite shift to Perring.

He was an unimaginative man and her hastily concocted tale of some article left in the car had seemed reasonable to him. He also volunteered the telephone number. For a few days she had fought down a desire to talk to Perring and then by the Friday night she could withstand the urge no longer. She had to see him alone and rather than give him the opportunity to say no, and she was sure he would deny her the admittedly dangerous act of visiting him at his flat, she had decided to call unannounced the next morning.

*   *   *

Dropping Jennings was easy enough. As she already knew

the man had little imagination and her decision to go shopping in Kings Road on a busy hot Saturday morning had not seemed odd to him. She left him to sit in the cafe at Peter Jones' while she ostensibly went to try on dresses. The security man seemed content and slightly relieved. Janet knew she could not risk being away too long. An hour, perhaps a little longer, but certainly no more than an hour and a half before even the guard became alarmed.

*   *   *

She walked quickly down the road that in the second half of the seventies looked very much as it had looked in the sixties when it had become synonymous with the kind of life style that had passed her by, but which now, belatedly she was reaching out to grasp. The houses in Flood Street were old and tall and beautifully restored. From outside the one where Perring had his flat was no different to the others, it did not look as if it had been turned into flats. The outer door had to be opened by a huge centrally placed brass knob before she could see the group of six press-buttons alongside six two-way speakers. She pressed the button beside his name and waited, tense in case he was out. He wasn't.

" Yes?" The voice was muffled but she felt her stomach lurch with recognition.

" John, it's me, Janet." The silence was long and she felt in that instant the foolishness of what she was doing.

" Come up." The door lock clicked and she went through the second door and hurried up the stairs.

*   *   *

Perring had hoped, vainly as it turned out, that she would not attempt to visit him until the job was over. Then it would not matter as he would either be moved on or he

119

would have found a way out of the predicament he now realised fully. The predicament of being in love. In love with the wife of a Minister of the government of what was for him a foreign power. The situation was ludicrous and he knew it and he knew he had to stop it. But knowing it was of little use. When he had heard Janet Ainsley's voice on the intercom he had felt the thrill that he had begun to experience on every occasion when they met. He pressed the release button and walked quickly over to the window. There were the usual cars parked nose to tail and only two people on foot, together and both in their early twenties. He went back to the door and put the lock on the latch.

*　　*　　*

When Janet walked into the room all thoughts they had shared at the danger of what they were doing disappeared.

" I'm sorry. I had to see you alone. I couldn't wait any longer."

Perring drew her to him and kissed her long and gently on the mouth.

" Janet my darling, don't say anything. I know . . . I know what it's been like. It's been the same for me."

" Has it? Has it really? You don't have to say that just to keep me happy. I'm too old to expect miracles and it's enough for me to know I love you."

" It isn't enough for me. And you're not too old for anything." He stopped suddenly as a thought struck him. " Jennings, where is he?"

" He's in the store at the end of the road. He thinks I'm in the dress department trying on clothes. He won't suspect. Not for an hour at least."

" An hour? It isn't long."

" It's long enough. Please. Let's go to bed now. Now."

Perring was already responding to the pressure of her body

120

against his and there was no further hesitation as he led her into the bedroom that adjoined the living room.

*　　*　　*

Like the first time they had been together neither wanted to waste time on preliminaries. Perring drew the curtains that overlooked the street outside and when he turned back from the window Janet was already half undressed, her slim figure softly lit by the sunlight that glowed through the red drapes. Perring started to take off his clothes and as she dropped the last garment to the floor Janet turned to him. They stood for a moment in the middle of the bedroom floor looking at and gently touching each other's body. Perring drew her towards the bed and then stopped as he felt the unexpected resistance. He turned his head and looked at her in surprise. She was smiling at him.

" Lie down. Please." He lay down on his back on the bed as he was asked and watched as Janet lay beside him. At first he could feel only her long hair as it brushed against his chest then he felt the slightest tingle as her lips began to caress his stomach. Involuntarily he tensed and then relaxed as her lips increased their pressure. He felt her touch move lower and then suddenly leave him to rejoin on his thighs. This time her gentle movement was upwards and he let his body respond to her as it wanted. When finally her warm moist mouth encircled him he knew he was close to climaxing and started to sit up.

" No, stop, I'm going to . . ."

" I want you to."

" But you, I won't be able to make love to you. Not in the time we have." She moved on the bed and looked down into his eyes.

" I don't mind. I want you in me, in every part of me." He put his arms around her and kissed her. Then before he could change his position she had slipped from his encircling arms to take him again into her mouth. This time he made no attempt to hold back, letting himself be brought to his orgasm in only seconds.

*   *   *

Afterwards he slowly regained his control and lifted her from where she lay, her lips and tongue still caressing him.

" I love you," he told her. For the first time he wondered at the limitations of the words. He had used them before, many times in similar situations, when he had spent himself in that or other ways, but never before had he meant it. He need not have worried that the words might not carry the weight he wanted them to. Something must have shown in the tone of his voice for Janet pressed herself to him urgently.

" I know you do," she whispered, " I thought at first you just wanted me for, well for what we've just done but I can feel it's different now. I love you too. You know that." She stopped speaking for a moment and they lay silently there and he could feel her heart beat against his chest and the beat was faster and more erratic than his own. After a moment he turned towards her.

" It's not going to be easy. Getting away together. It will be almost as bad for me as for you."

" I know it will be hard. I'm prepared for that. What do you want me to do?"

" I'm not sure. There will be an uproar. It will damage your husband's career however we do it. You don't want that do you."

" Not if it can be avoided but if it can't then we will have to live with whatever happens to him."

" Can you divorce him without me coming into it? The newspapers would love it wouldn't they? You and your body-
122

guard, a security man on your husband's own staff."

"I don't know, I haven't thought about it. Can we meet again soon? In the next few days. We can decide what we are going to do. Can we?" Perring thought for a few moments.

"I'm on duty tomorrow and Tuesday. You have the dinners for the Heads of State every evening."

"Yes but Tuesday I'm free in the morning. All morning until after lunch. We can do what I did today. I can go shopping and you will automatically go with me. We can come here. We can be together for five or six hours." For an instant Perring felt the warning tremors he had experienced earlier in their relationship. He had never inclined towards self-examination. He had no idea what made him tick although he was aware enough to know that the men who employed him did know. The affair with Janet Ainsley had changed him in several ways and that was one of them, now he thought over the situation all the time, trying constantly to understand his own state of mind.

* * *

That he should fall in love for the first time with a woman he had been ordered to seduce was something he found almost unbelievable. What his employers would say if they found out did not bear thinking about. For a short while he toyed with the thought that he should tell them himself, ask for their understanding. In that day-dream they would agree to let him and Janet go away together. He knew the idea was ridiculous but it stayed there below the surface of his mind and it helped to make bearable the hours he was alone thinking. As for the minutes he was with Janet, then the thought helped him to maintain an appearance that all was well and would continue to remain so. He knew it was futile but the game had to be played that way, he could not let her know, both because he loved her and because he was afraid to seriously consider, the probable end to it all.

*　　*　　*

He was also thinking more about Stellman. He had no idea when Stellman planned to act. He decided it was not likely to be before Tuesday and he agreed to her suggestion that they should meet on that day. There was no logical reasoning in his opinion that Stellman would not act before that day, just a guess that he was not yet ready coupled with a desire to spend more time alone with Janet before they were plunged into what would very probably prove to be a hard and difficult period. It would also be dangerous but that was something else he did not want to think too much about.

*　　*　　*

In a room on the top floor of the French Embassy in London a young woman sat waiting to be briefed on her next assignment. She was restless, eager to be gone from the building where the polite formality contrasted grotesquely with the kind of work she did for her country. It made her more aware of what she had become. At moments like that she wondered at the depths of her patriotism. Then she thought about the man she had met in the bar at the Inn On The Park and she knew from what had happened that night that her patriotism must be bottomless.

A door opened and a tall man came out to her from an inner room.

" Please come in."

She followed him into the room and looked incuriously at the short man seated at a desk that appeared too large for him. Her expression of indifference was a mask and she knew it and he knew it too. No one was indifferent to him.

Everyone who knew him had real feelings, either hatred or fear and often both. For the first time she could remember he was smiling.

"Sit down my dear," he told her, "you did very well, you are to be congratulated. Tell me what happened." She knew he had read her detailed report and she knew he was not looking for voyeuristic titillation. He wanted to be certain there was nothing she had omitted from her report.

"I was in the bar at the hotel on Park Lane. I was there to meet my contact at the Russian Embassy. I saw this man come in and I recognised him. He was at a conference I attended in Berlin a few years ago. I could remember nothing about him but I had . . . well I had an intuitive feeling."

"Do not deny your intuition my dear, it is an extra sense we all should have. Go on."

"He had several drinks and I let him pick me up. My Russian contact came in, saw I was involved and left. I went with the man, he told me his name was John Perring, to his flat. I thought of using a drug but he seemed to need to talk and with all the drink he had it was easy. I think the material can be relied upon."

"I think so too. Very good, you have done well." The man behind the desk paused and the girl looked at his hands, stubby and densely covered in black hairs. They touched and the fingers wound together into a hairy ball. Surprised she realised he was nervous, no that wasn't it, uncomfortable. He coughed and looked up at her.

"I, none of us are unaware of the . . . the difficulties of being a woman in this business. Do not think we are unappreciative or unsympathetic. You are due for a change of scene. We have an operation coming up in the Mediterranean, it will be an easy job for you. You will be able to rest, you need it. You leave tomorrow."

He waved one of the little hairy hands at her and she felt a touch on her elbow. The tall man took her outside to the outer room before she had time to say anything. In the silence of the room she looked up at the tall man.

" I . . ."

" You are surprised. He is a surprising man. Most people hate him, or fear him. Those of us who know him well know better." He glanced sideways at her and she knew he had not really stated he did not still fear the little man. She nodded and walked to the door.

*   *   *

After he had seen the woman out the tall man returned to the inner office. The small man looked up at him.

" I think we have it all."

" I agree."

" She is good. We must use her more often. This rest will do her good. Now what about Perring."

" Interesting. We can certainly use the information about the Ainsley woman. I'm not sure what to make of the rest of it."

" Neither am I. I confess to being rather confused. As far as we know Perring is not a killer. He seems to be a rather weak man, a womaniser and unreliable. I have always been surprised that he was used so much. He is unlikely to be used in an important role."

" Perhaps not. But he could have a supporting role to someone who is important, someone who can allow for and correct any errors Perring might make."

" I take it we can assume that whatever he is in London for has some relationship to the conference."

" That might be too much too assume. He has been here a long time according to the information we have obtained since the girl met him. It is however not unreasonable to as-sume that he is now being used by someone who is here to act in some way that connects with the conference."

126

"I agree that is an assumption that is reasonable in the circumstances. We shall act on it. I want a tail on Perring. Full, round the clock watch. Report on everything he does and more important everyone he meets."

"Very well." The tall man turned and left the room leaving the small man staring thoughtfully at the opposite wall.

*   *   *

Stellman had watched the woman ring the bell at the house in Flood Street with an expression of surprise on his normally bland face. He had recognised her immediately. His preparatory work before any job invariably included committing to memory photographs of every person within touching distance. He had to know who people were in order that as the time for the job drew nearer he could assess their likely effect upon the work he was doing. The photographs he had studied for this job included every member of the visiting heads of state's official entourage. Any others he saw with them he could then conclude were either interpreters or security men. For his purpose he would conclude they were the latter. That way he would not relax his guard. As far as the host government was concerned he memorised all members of the British cabinet and in case he had decided to do the job on a social occasion he had studied pictures of the wives of all cabinet members. Janet Ainsley had stood out as an extraordinarily attractive woman and he had half guessed her reason for being at the house before he saw Perring draw the curtains at the window of what Stellman confidently assumed to be the bedroom. His reason for being outside the flat in Flood Street had, until then, no ominous meaning. He had driven into the street simply to ensure he knew the layout in case he had to call in a hurry. Now he knew he would be calling. It was a pity, it would increase the number of risks he would be taking. At least he would not have to clear things with his employers. When they asked why he would tell them what Perring was doing and they would be pleased that a security risk had been removed.

He started the car and drove out into the main road. He was reasonably content. He had everything he needed. The hardware Perring had supplied was all in perfect working order and he was confident it would all do what he wanted of it. The additional hardware he had needed, about which Perring knew nothing, had been easy to obtain. He had not believed the assurances he had received before he left the island. He could not believe that it was possible to buy openly in English shops so many of the raw materials for mayhem. In America they accepted the open sale of firearms and he knew the English did not accept it. They could not understand the American need for weaponry. And so they did not permit its sale in their own country. But they did nothing to stop the sale of articles which alone were harmless but which added together formed a weapon deadlier and more unstable than a rifle or revolver.

*   *   *

He turned the car west along Kings Road and decided to recheck the layout at the pub on the Kingston By-Pass. He had satisfied himself of the best route for the motorcade leaving the American Embassy and he had sent a message through to the Sleeper to ensure the route was taken at the appropriate time. All he could do now was wait and already he was tense with the expectancy of the job facing him. He had already decided that driving would help and rather than an aimless tour it seemed useful to look again at the place where he planned to meet the man Perring was providing. The traffic thinned as he drove and he was soon crossing the river into Putney.

*   *   *

Comoy gave permission for the real destination of Air Force One to be announced at ten o'clock. He knew the Prime Minister and the rest of the party due to meet the President would be irritated and he also knew they would quickly understand and forgive the change to their plans.

*   *   *

As soon as the telephone calls had been made he went down to the cars drawn up in array and climbed into the lead Cadillac.

" Okay Bill, south down the A3," he told the driver. He turned and grinned slightly at Harry Walters who was sitting at the back with Frank Hunt. " Down to your part of the world."

" I thought we were going to Heathrow."

" So, we hope, does everyone else."

" Where then?"

" About six miles this side of Guildford there's a strip. One of your manufacturers uses it as a test-flight field. The President's jet is coming in there." Walters was silent for a few minutes as the car sped along the crowded streets.

"Not my place I suppose but I must ask. Why?" he asked the small dark American.

" Why? Heathrow is too vulnerable. So is any big airport. Whatever you do, apart from closing the damn place down, there are too many people around."

" Yes I realise that. That isn't what I meant. At least from Heathrow you're exposed there and on the route into the city. This way you're safe at the airfield but you will have the President open to attack for much longer on the road."

" Agreed, but we have the advantage that anyone planning an attempt on the President's life will not know where we

129

are until it is too late to plan anything." Walters sat back and thought more about it. He decided he would have preferred the shorter car journey from west London but he kept his ideas to himself. Comoy had the experience after all. He stared out of the window as the car wound through the traffic on the south side of the river and headed towards the Kingston By-Pass. No one in the lead Cadillac or in any other car in the procession took particular note of the white Ford Cortina. It was just another car among many.

*   *   *

Stellman however took a great deal of notice of the cars that passed him. He had put two and two together within seconds and he decided to go along for the ride at least for a few miles. It was obvious some change of plan had taken place. He knew Leeson was due in at Heathrow and while there was a good road from where they were to the airport it was not the way someone starting from Grosvenor Square would travel. He thought it would be interesting to see how the opposition was thinking.

*   *   *

He followed the cars for several miles past the point where he had been headed. When he was certain they were not going to Heathrow even by the most circuitous route imaginable he fell back and turned off into a side road. He knew there was no large airport on that road. Gatwick was the only other one in the South of England and they were not going there. It had to be a military base or a civil airlines maintenance field. He turned back and drove north towards the hotel. Wherever the President was coming in he was faced with a long drive in a motor car. Even though a moving car was a difficult target even for an experienced marksman there was little defence against a determined bomber. That

130

meant that whoever was running the security operation had something on his mind.

Exchanging the brief dangers of Heathrow for the protracted ones of a forty miles or longer drive suggested that either the security man was an idiot or he had wind of something. Stellman knew that whoever was in charge he would not be an idiot. That meant there was suspicion that an attempt was to be made on the President's life. He realised the direction his thoughts were taking him and he deliberately relaxed himself. He was leaping to conclusions. They were just being ultra cautious. No one could know what he was there for. No one could know he was there or who he was.

*　　*　　*

He turned into the car park at the Marquis of Granby. He stopped the car and looked around. It would do very well. Very well indeed. He felt suddenly hungry and climbed out of the car. The hotel looked a pleasant place to eat and he had a sense of challenge in eating calmly in a place he was soon to project into the headlines.

*　　*　　*

The Cadillac turned left off the main road and followed by the other cars drove down towards the airfield. Walters saw, with growing astonishment, signs of the incredible organisation Comoy had at his fingertips. There were armed American soldiers everywhere. Outnumbering them were the police. Walters recognised several faces among the uniformed men from his own county force.

"Do you mean no one knew where we were going until an hour ago?" he asked Comoy.

"No. They were alert for instructions but we didn't tell

them where."

"What about them?" Walters pointed to a party of heavily armed American troops.

"They are from the various Air Force bases we have here. They were gathered into the area ready to head for Heathrow. It didn't cause many problems to redirect them here instead." The car swung round to stop in front of a hangar and the other cars drew up in formation. Comoy climbed out and the others followed. A slightly harassed looking man descended on them.

"Mr. Comoy?"

"That's me. You will be Mr. Bennett."

"Yes that's correct."

"Everything going well?"

"Yes I suppose so." Bennett looked uneasily across the tarmacadamed area in front of the hangar and shook his head. "Not what we're used to you know."

"No I realise that. It will soon be over. When is the aircraft due to land?"

"Forty-five minutes. Who . . . who is on it?" Before anyone could answer the second group of cars appeared and drove over to where the others were parked. The door of the second car opened and Charles Fox stepped out. Bennett looked at him in amazement. He turned to Walters who was nearest to him.

"Then it's President Leeson's aircraft?" Walters glanced at Comoy for guidance. Comoy nodded easily at Bennett.

"Correct Mr. Bennett. The plane we're here for is Air Force One. The Presidential aircraft."

"I'd better get back to the control room," Bennett said. He hurried away a man suddenly more important than he had been for years. Walters looked at Hunt.

"Was that wise? He could call someone. The press maybe." The colonel grinned and shook his head.

"No he couldn't. We're manning the telephone and we

132

have someone supervising all radios." He pointed. " There's Commissioner Adams. I expect he is the one most likely to want to throw a fit. We made this change without reference to him." He walked over to the Commissioner followed by Walters. Comoy had temporarily disappeared. Adams did not look like a man about to throw a fit. He smiled at the two men as they approached him.

" Colonel. Inspector. Good afternoon gentlemen. I see you are well organised Colonel."

" Yes sir. I expect you are wondering why . . ."

" No Colonel I'm not. I must admit I was unhappy about Heathrow myself. This is better although the ride back into London may cause us a few problems at such short notice. However if you have done this in such a short time the least we can do is to ensure a safe return trip." He glanced at Walters and followed the direction of the Inspector's eyes.

* * *

The Home Secretary was standing near a small group of men that included the Prime Minister and the Foreign Secretary and the United States Ambassador. He looked desperately ill and Adams sensed what was going through Walters mind.

" Inspector," he said quietly and drew the younger man aside, " remember you did what was right. Absolutely right."

" I know that sir but, well, look at him. It's a miracle the press hasn't guessed already."

Adams studied the slight figure and he felt a small stirring of something indefinable inside him. What his wife called his one streak of femininity, his intuition. Walters had been right in the way his mind had taken the Home Secretary's appearance. He was looking worse than he should. True he had suffered a severe shock, his wife and daughter injured, badly injured. That on top of the pressures that were already breaking him were enough, too much for almost any man.

133

But there was something else, a haunted look that had not been there before. Before the Minister had maintained a surface expression of calm assuredness. Something had changed. Perhaps Evans knew the police were investigating him, perhaps he had found out about the tape recordings. Could there be anything else? There was nothing to be done then but Adams knew he had to check on the possibility of other things when he got back to London.

*   *   *

Precisely on time the aircraft carrying the President of the United States of America touched down on the runway. The Prime Minister went on board to greet the President and within a few minutes the two men came briskly down the steps. With no newsmen or tv cameras to delay the proceedings the customary speeches and guards of honour were dispensed with and soon everyone was being shepherded into the waiting cars. The President and the Prime Minister were in the back of the Cadillac Comoy and Hunt and Walters had travelled down in. This time Comoy and Hunt occupied the extra seats in the rear compartment. A tall taciturn man sat in the front seat beside the driver.

"We meet again Lewis," the President said in his high-pitched voice.

"Yes sir." There was a short silence as Comoy looked into the slightly protuberant eyes of the President and thought how much he disliked the man from Wisconsin. As always however he kept his face studiously blank. Apart from one occasion he had never let his opinions be known. On that one occasion he mentioned his dislike to a colleague and had countered the other man's questioning look with a half-joking reference to the earlier politician from the same state. The colleague had asked pointedly if Comoy really thought the President could be talked of in the same breath as Joseph

134

McCarthy and Comoy had never discussed his feelings about David Leeson with anyone else since. Now, physically closer to the President than he had been for a long time, he felt all the old dislikes flooding back as strongly as ever.

"I got your message," the President said. In the silence that followed Comoy felt Hunt tense beside him but he let nothing show in his face. Sitting as he was, facing both the President and the British Prime Minister, he could not risk a warning glance. Instead he nodded slowly.

"I'm pleased you did sir, it shows communications are working if nothing else." The deliberately casual answer had the effect he wanted. Leeson changed the subject.

"How long does this route take to the embassy?"

"A little over an hour Mr. President," Hunt answered obviously relieved that the conversation had taken a safer course.

"Well let's not waste the time. Anything we can talk about Mr. Prime Minister, anything not too classified for these gentlemen?" Comoy felt his colour begin to rise and he glanced quickly at the Englishman. He was pleased to see a mildly concerned expression there. Fox had not missed the antagonism the President was showing towards the security man.

"I'm sure we can Mr. President." Fox answered. "For example there is the problem of the arms sales in West Africa. That is as open as any state secret can be."

*　　*　　*

Comoy relaxed as the two men began to discuss the recently announced sales of arms by a Scandinavian country to an emergent state on the Atlantic coast of Africa. He let his mind drift onto other problems closer to himself.

*　　*　　*

It was nearing four in the afternoon when the Cadillac turned into Park Lane. Comoy sat up straighter and looked keenly out of the rear and side windows. Regardless of the point of arrival for the aircraft everyone knew the Heads of State were all staying at their own Embassies and a potential assassin could very well have decided that simply lurking in the general vicinity of Grosvenor Square was an effective way of getting close to the President.

*   *   *

The cars swung into the outer lane and made the turn at the Brook Gate traffic lights leading into Upper Brook Street. They were within yards of the rear of the American Embassy when the small van came out of Park Street at right angles to the line they were following. The policemen on permanent duty in the area around the Embassy had stopped traffic at the radio announcement that the motorcade was approaching. The two men placed at the junction leaped aside as the van roared towards them. Comoy had a clear impression of the vehicle and it was an immeasurable moment of time before the fact that it was driverless registered in his mind.

*   *   *

Afterwards he could not remember clearly what had happened and Colonel Hunt had to tell him that he had reached across and opened the nearside door of the Cadillac and in one fluid movement he had pushed the Prime Minister from the car and then seizing the President's arm he had thrown himself after the Englishman dragging David Leeson with him. He did remember the crash as the van had struck the offside of the Cadillac and none of them ever forgot the shattering roar as the van exploded turning itself and the Embassy limousine into a blazing inferno.

136

SEVEN

Stellman heard the news of the bombing in the television room at the hotel. He had taken to spending time in there in the late evenings. The tension he felt as the time for the job drew nearer left him edgy and irritable and too much time spent alone in his room only made things worse. The dark anonymity of the room helped. No one could see him particularly well and the programmes, whatever they were, took his mind from ceaselessly nagging over details.

* * *

He had returned leisurely from his run out into the country and had eaten alone in a Chinese restaurant where the customary and deliberately observed failure of communication prevented idle conversation. He had been unprepared for the news and when the programme came on dealing matter of factly with something that had obviously been covered in detail earlier in the evening he sat shocked and disbelieving in the darkness, the announcer's voice passing almost unnoticed through his consciousness.

* * *

Covering all eventualities was an automatic process yet the thought of another assassination attempt had never occurred to him. He had not covered that. The likely result could be catastrophic. Any change in the security procedures would destroy his carefully laid plans. And there was no time left. He was due to leave the country on the package holiday flight on Wednesday at midday. Today was Saturday, almost Sunday. He could not possibly reorganise in the time. There was only one course open to him. The Sleeper would have to ensure the procedures were not changed. If he could.

He went up to his bedroom and lay sleepless on the bed for several hours before his mind had cooled to its normal level. That was when he realised he could do nothing and therefore worrying was a wasted effort. If the Sleeper could help he would already be doing so. If he could not there was an end to it. The job would have to be abandoned. He would proceed as if all was going as planned. If it did the job would be done. If it did not he would be one million three hundred thousand worse off. He grinned slightly in the darkness at the thought. He could remember the day when he could not even count that far let alone have that much money.

*　　*　　*

He turned over to sleep and his last thought before drifting into dreamless rest was to wonder how the news of the bombing would have affected Perring.

*　　*　　*

Perring had heard the news much earlier than Stellman. Although off-duty the visit of Janet Ainsley had unsettled him and he had gone down to the office to see if there was anything he could do that would occupy his mind. He had been eagerly snapped up by the hard pressed duty commander and in minutes he had found himself in a fast car streaking down the road towards Guildford. He gathered from the others in the car that a late change in plans had been made and the expected arrival point of the President had been moved from Heathrow to the BAC landing strip near Ripley.

*   *   *

Once there he had automatically drifted into the group of security men he knew best, those who were with the Foreign Secretary. After the President's aircraft had landed Perring had stayed with Ainsley and when the Foreign Secretary and the American Secretary of State Arnold Perryman had climbed into the car Ainsley had used for the outward trip Perring got in with them.

*   *   *

The motorcade had stayed together for the drive back to London but once in the central area it had begun to split up, the various drivers obviously following a laid-down pattern. The car Perring was in had stayed behind the car carrying the President and the Prime Minister until they were in Knightsbridge. There the leading group had slid into the left hand slip road that took them along Hyde Park Corner and towards the turn into Park Lane while the following group stayed on the main road and went into the underpass connecting Knightsbridge with Piccadilly.

*   *   *

No one in the Foreign Secretary's car heard the explosion. They were too far away for that but within seconds they heard the emergency messages pouring from the radio. The driver automatically accelerated away from the other evening traffic, switching on the seldom used siren as he did so. Perring was too busy with his thoughts to react correctly.

139

Although there was no doubt something had happened he did not know what. The messages on the radio were instructional not informative and nothing was said that indicated what had happened.

Had there been an attempt on the President's or the Prime Minister's life? And if there had been an attempt had Stellman done it? If he had then it was a completely different plan to the one Perring had assumed was being made. Stellman had never taken him into his confidence but the questions he had asked about routes from the Embassy to the Conference Centre had all led Perring to assume that the job, whatever it was, and it seemed obvious to him it was to be an assassination, was planned for when the President's car was on that journey and it would not make that journey until Monday morning.

*   *   *

Very slowly he began to panic. Knowing very little about the job Stellman was there to do, had been unsettling all along. That Stellman appeared to be keeping his plans even more under cover made him feel very vulnerable. He felt a hand on his arm. The second security officer in the car was shaking him and shouting at the driver.

"For Christ's sake slow down. And cut off that siren. We don't want all the attention we're getting. And stay on the route we planned." Perring forced himself to take an interest. The comments of the other man were sound. The car was unmarked and was not likely to draw attention. And by staying on the determined route their passage was known by the men at the other end of the radio.

Ainsley leaned forward towards Perring.

"What can you make out? Have they said what has happened?"

"No sir. There has obviously been an attack of some kind

140

on the cars that were with the President and the Prime Minister. Nothing has been said that suggests it was their car that was the subject but we can assume it is."

"I think we had better get over there," the Secretary of State put in. A small nervous looking man he had a fearsome reputation as a hard negotiator and a tireless worker at lost causes. The nervous manner, Perring realised, was just that, a mannerism and nothing more. A frightened man would not have suggested going near the Embassy.

"No sir. Not yet. There will be congestion over there. We might get stuck and we would be a sitting target. We go where we planned and once we are there we can find out what has happened and decide what needs doing." The American nodded slowly and leaned back in the seat. Perring looked at Ainsley and for the first time since he had made love to Janet Ainsley he looked into the other man's eyes. He saw nothing there that could cause him concern. Indeed the expression there was that of a man tired but alert, and unafraid. For a moment Perring felt a small surge of unaccustomed fellow feeling for the older man. Then he quelled it. Ainsley was not only the husband of the woman he loved he was also a Minister in the government of a foreign power. There were no grounds on which they could meet.

*   *   *

Of the six men in the Cadillac two were dead. Comoy's quick reactions had saved his own life and the lives of the President and the Prime Minister. Swept along on his coattails had been Colonel Hunt.

"I saw you going Lewis and, well, I just went with you. I didn't stop to think why."

"The others?" Comoy was sitting in an Embassy office drinking a cup of tea and wishing it was brandy. He couldn't stop his hands from shaking and he was disgusted with himself for that. No one else was disgusted with him. Already the President and the Prime Minister, neither of whom had suffered more than minor abrasions from hitting the roadway, had been to see him and to thank him.

Comoy had been less fortunate. He had landed on his head and as the explosion had roared in his ears he had lost consciousness. Hunt had got away with grazes and bruises and superficial burns from the burning fuel that had spattered the area.

" The others didn't make it," the colonel answered regretfully, " the driver was just too slow in moving and the guy in the passenger seat, what was his name, Youngman, he never stood a chance. The van hit the nearside front of the car and he must have died instantly."

Comoy nodded and rubbed his eyes with his free hand.

" What do we know?"

" Very little. The Commissioner is in charge out there. I left him to it. That's his kind of job and it is his territory."

" I expect you're right. Still we can't sit here." Comoy stood up and at that moment the door opened. " Commissioner, we were just coming to see what was happening." Adams sat down and after a moment's hesitation Comoy sat down again.

" Not much. We know what happened and that's about all. The van was in the area on apparently legitimate business. Making deliveries, it had been cleared and the driver had been screened. Not too well it begins to seem. Someone had built a very effective and very damaging weapon out of it. High explosives in the body of the van with a small charge inside the engine compartment. It was all set up to detonate on impact. And for good measure there was also a fire bomb in there."

" How was it fixed so it would drive itself? I take it I wasn't dreaming when I saw there was no driver."

" No there wasn't. They lined it up and aimed it then

142

locked the wheel in some way. There are pieces of what looks like a clamp in the wreckage."

"Lined it up how for God's sake? Why didn't anyone see it? They can't have done that in a few seconds. It must have taken time."

"I don't know the answers Mr. Comoy but I will before many more hours have passed."

"I take it you haven't found anyone?"

"No. No one. Needless to say the entire area is sealed off. But it isn't easy." Comoy nodded slowly. He knew it wasn't easy and more he knew there was another underlying problem that no one had touched upon. But after a moment's silence the Commissioner did touch upon it.

"Do you think this was your man?" Comoy sat silently for a moment.

He looked at the other two men. Then he shook his head.

"No. It's all wrong. If he is who we think he is this is out of style."

"How do you know?"

"What?"

"How do you know it is out of style? If he was involved in Dallas maybe that was out of style, maybe this is his usual method of operation. Maybe he simply changes his style to suit the operation he has in mind. There isn't enough to go on." Comoy stood up again and winced at the pain in his head.

"Dammit Frank isn't there any brandy here?" Hunt grinned slightly and spoke softly into a telephone.

"On its way. The Commissioner has something there Lewis. We don't know enough to make guesses."

"We know so damned little all we can do is make guesses." For a moment some of Comoy's accumulated frustrations showed in his voice. A knock at the door stopped all discussion and Hunt opened it to take the brandy bottle and three glasses. He poured two small measures and one large one for Comoy. The dark man took the glass noting with some satisfaction that his hand had stopped shaking. He drank half the contents of the glass and then looked at the others. " Okay. If you're right and it was him then he may try again. If I'm right and it wasn't him then he will still be trying. We stay as we are. We assume there will be another attempt."

" I didn't suggest we should drop our guard."

" No Commissioner I know you didn't but there will be a reaction among the men. A reaction towards carelessness, it's quite commonplace in a situation like this. They think, subconsciously, that it's all over and they start relaxing. I've seen it happen before. It musn't happen this time."

" It won't." Adams stood up and looked down at the others. " We may have an internal problem to worry about."

" What's that?"

" Someone knew the Presidential car was coming into Grosvenor Square by that route. They didn't set that mobile bomb up in Park Street on the off-chance. That is a co-incidence I won't believe." The two Americans looked at one another as the tall policeman left.

" He has a point Lewis. Again."

" Maybe." Comoy thought for a moment. " What is happening upstairs?"

" The President and the Prime Minister are talking. When the first excitement has died down Mr. Fox will be going back to Downing Street. The President has no engagements for today. He's staying inside." " Thank God for that anyway." Comoy held out his glass and the Colonel filled it again but this time with a normal measure. After a moment's hesitation he refilled his own glass.

" Where do we go from here?" he asked Comoy.

" We start by checking out all staff who had access to today's route. Mind you, there is always the point that it would take only a reasonably intelligent guess to reckon

144

that we would enter the Embassy environs by that route. Off Park Lane into Upper Brook Street and into the yard at the back of the Embassy."

" So we check everybody?"

" Looks like it."

" If it was our friend and if he did set it all up then he has help. He needed access to the man who had the permit to be in the area and he needed to buy gelignite and God knows what else."

" Help can be bought."

" Like he must have bought it in Dallas?"

" What are you getting at Frank?"

" You know there are several schools of thought about what really happened there? Well, leaving out the lunatic element what have we? Two basic choices. Either our friend did it and set up Oswald as a dummy to take the rap which he did. Or Oswald did do it and our friend set up things so he couldn't miss."

" You mean he might be here to set things up and is using whatever tools are at his disposal. Like there he was given Oswald who could use a rifle at long range but was probably too dumb to set things up in the right way and here he has been given people who like to play with bombs?"

" It's a thought."

" No Frank, it might be a thought but it isn't one I like. It's too . . . too speculative. Dallas was tidy. No mess."

" Oswald's arrest was a mess. And what happened afterwards."

" Maybe but up to that point, up to the point when Oswald left the building it was as close to a perfect job of its kind as you are likely to get. Our man is a planner. Bombs are not for planners. They are for people who are not sure. Bombs can kill with near misses, or they can fail to kill with a hit."

" Like this one."

"Precisely. Even with a hit on the car they still missed their target. That isn't our friend's style. It isn't, Frank. It wasn't him. I'm sure of it. He's still out there and whatever it is he is planning is still in the pipeline. Believe me I'm sure of it."

*　　*　　*

Few of the people directly and indirectly involved in the security operation slept that night. Few of the men high in the governments of the United Kingdom and the United States of America slept either. Meetings went on behind closed and in many cases locked doors until the early hours of Sunday morning. The details released to the press had been deliberately garbled. The explosion could not be dismissed. What had been changed was the identity of the passengers in the Cadillac. The press were told that the car had contained security men, two of whom had died. The car carrying the President and the Prime Minister, they were told, had escaped the attack by several minutes. Hardly anyone among the hordes of pressmen who flocked to the area believed what they were told but they could not get near enough to see which car had been involved and they could not get anyone to answer their questions. All they had was the statement issued by Commissioner Adams. They were very unhappy about it but there was nothing they could do.

*　　*　　*

By the middle of Sunday morning Hunt had come round to Comoy's line of thought. He agreed that the chances were the attempt had been something completely outside what the man from the motel had planned. They very nearly convinced Adams but he still retained some of his earlier scepticism.

146

"In any case," he added, before putting an end to the three-way telephone conversation, "if this was another party altogether maybe it will throw your man out of his stride. That might help us."

"That man," remarked the Colonel, "is getting too damned clever in his comments. Doesn't he ever say anything that doesn't seem reasonable and right?" Comoy grinned for the first time since the explosion.

"He isn't paid to guess wrong, and for that matter neither are we. Let's review the plans for the week's meetings."

"I've talked to the President. He doesn't want any changes. He had a long talk last night with Fox and they want everything left as it is. They don't want to alarm the others."

"Good."

"Good?"

"It lets us off one particular hook. We don't have to tell the foreign security groups about our unknown friend. If Leeson wants this kept under wraps then he would certainly want that keeping quiet."

"Your guessing Lewis. If Leeson knew what we think, if he knew about the print and about Dallas he would be . . ."

"Finish the sentence Frank. He would be a scared rabbit."

"What exactly did you say in the message you sent him?"

"Just that I felt the security shield we could give him here was inadequate."

"That doesn't seem to have frightened him so why should the other?"

"It's different Frank. An inadequate security operation is nebulous, you can't be afraid of it. But Dallas is a reality that is right there in the mind of all our politicians. Particularly in any President's mind. And when the President is a man like Leeson . . ."

147

" I don't understand you. I never did. Why, if you dislike the man as much as you seem to do, you stay in the job? He knows you dislike him and he'd be glad to see you go."

" It's the job I get paid to do. Protecting the President is part of it. Not the man. The holder of the office. I can't expect to like the man every time. Since we formed the Department I've only worked for two. Singer and Leeson. I liked Singer and I agreed with his politics. I don't like Leeson and I don't like his politics."

" Which comes first? Disliking the man or his politics?"

" That's a coincidence Frank. No, it really is. I wouldn't like Leeson's brand of politics if he was Prince Charming himself. All he does is pretty the surface of a dirty and vicious pool of reactionary thinking. He is a John Bircher in party dress. And you know it as well as I do."

" Maybe I do. But I don't say it. And neither should you. You've said enough in the last few minutes to get you fired ten times over. And probably enough to get you arraigned at least once. I think we should leave it Lewis. Let's put it down to the crack on the head."

" Don't worry about it Frank. Washington know how I feel. They didn't fire me when Leeson won three years ago because they knew I was the best man for the job. They won't fire me now because I'm still the best. But you are right, let's drop it. Not for your reasons, because we have work to do. If everything goes ahead as planned let's make sure what we have is as tight as possible."

* * *

Raymond Adams returned to his office after satisfying himself there was nothing he could do that would advance the investigations in Grosvenor Square. He was vaguely conscious that he was doing what the American Comoy had said was to be feared. He was relaxing his guard. If the man at the motel had been a potential assassin then the assassination attempt the previous day was probably his work. He knew Comoy did not agree but equally he felt that a separate attempt was too much of a coincidence. In any event he had a great deal of work to do.

*　　*　　*

The investigation of the Home Secretary had proved to be as distasteful as he had expected. The investigation had to be carried out, he knew that, but nevertheless there was the distaste he felt at doing anything underhand. So far as he was able to determine there was nothing criminal in Peter Evans' activities, erratic yes and he did not doubt the parallel investigation by the Prime Minister's political watchdogs would have found more evidence of the unreliability the man's breakdown must have caused in his work. Knowing that Charles Fox intended requesting the Home Secretary's resignation immediately after the conference helped. Then the man would cease to be his immediate superior. In the meantime he had to continue and he had to do his best to ensure the press did not learn what was going on. He was helped in this in that most sections of the press and television companies were concentrating on the conference. If they did hear of the Home Secretary's mental instability their reaction would not be calm, particularly amongst those newspapers that supported the opposition. Adams rubbed his hand across his eyes. He hoped the conference would be a success and he hoped nothing else would arise that would cause political embarrassment. Catching criminals was sufficiently time-consuming, he didn't need anything else on top of that.

*　　*　　*

Michael Ainsley had found work impossible after the attempt on the Prime Minister's life. He had talked with Fox for a few minutes to satisfy himself that there had been no injuries then he had gone to his study to put the finishing touches to the many things he would be discussing at the opening meeting on Monday. But that was Monday and there was still Sunday to get through. Sunday and the arrival of the French, Russians and Chinese parties. For the first time for weeks he left his study and put aside thoughts of work for the night.

He had not dined alone with his wife for months. Not that he had been consciously aware of that until he sat facing her across the table. Almost at once he was aware of the change in her. For a start she seemed gayer, more alive. And she looked younger and lovelier than he could ever remember before.

There was nothing in their conversation to cause him any alarm. It dealt mostly with the meetings and dinners and lunches scheduled for the coming week but sometime during the meal he began to experience a feeling. He was barely aware of it at first but then it began to grow and even then it was long after the meal was over and he had returned in some confusion to the seclusion of his study that he was able to put a name to the feeling. He was suspicious, suspicious of his wife. Suspicious that Janet had . . . He stopped himself from thinking any further along the lines that had become distasteful. He had to be wrong but he could not allow himself to pursue the thought. Even so he decided that as soon as the conference was over he would arrange for enquiries, discreet enquiries, to be made. Then almost before that thought had had time to take root he knew he would not follow through with the plan to investigate his wife.

For one reason only, he did not want to know if his suspicions were right. He did not want to know if she was being unfaithful to him. Older than his wife by several years he had always kept under control the fear that some day the seemingly inevitable might happen. Perhaps that day had arrived and if it had he was defenceless against it. It was better therefore that he did not know.

*   *   *

The old man sat at the wide window watching the sun setting and the sky slowly darkening, the blackness broken by occasional flashes of brilliant colour as the sun's rays caught the edges of the few wispy evening clouds. He took no particular pleasure in the sight. He was waiting. He saw the glint of the headlights of the two cars as they approached down the long dusty road and he grunted and levered himself into an upright position and fumbled at the control box on the arm of his wheel chair. The chair spun round and drifted silently to the middle of the room.

*   *   *

The two men came into the room without knocking. The old man hated the waste of time and energy that created. The youngest man looked down at the old man and nodded a greeting. Little more ever passed between them. There was no need for greetings or for small talk. Neither had that kind of mind. The old man was pleased with his choice. He knew that when he died and the young man took control things would be in good hands. He turned his attention to the other man. He was tall and thin and wore glasses. He was about the same age as the stocky man he had replaced. The old man thought about that for a moment. A pity really, he had been a good man in many respects. Even the unauthorised report on the Sleeper that had caused his removal had been a good move. Good but unauthorised. And the old man could not afford to allow anyone to get away with open opposition to his authority. The two men sat down and waited. The young man composed, the thin bespectacled man nervous. He had not met the old man before.

"What happened?" The old man opened the meeting.

"We don't know."

"It wasn't Stellman?"

"No. He will not vary the plan. We know that."

"So there are others. That could prove awkward."

"It could."

"What have you done about it?"

"We have sent in a small team to find out what they can. With instructions to prevent any confusion developing that could obstruct Stellman."

"They have not been told Stellman is there?"

"Of course not." For an instant a note of asperity crept into the young man's voice. "They have simple instructions. Find the bombers and prevent further action."

"Good." The old man looked at the man who would succeed him from under hooded eyelids. The note of irritation had not escaped him. Then he dismissed it from his mind which was as near as he would ever come to admitting he had been in the wrong. He turned his attention to the second man who was sitting on the edge of his seat.

"What about Perring?"

"Everything is as the first report indicated. He is having an affair with the Ainsley woman." The old man snorted, the sound being both exclamation and censure of their agent.

"Has anything been done to correct matters?"

"No. We cannot risk affecting Stellman. He still needs Perring. We have decided to wait until Stellman has finished and left the country. After all . . ." He broke off.

"After all what?"

"It may be that Stellman has his own plans. He has a reputation for tidiness." The old man nodded slowly. It began to look as if he had selected a useful replacement.

Once he was over his nervousness the thin man would make a good foil to the younger man.

" So all is set for tomorrow?"

" Yes."

" Good. Everything set here? All statements prepared ready for issue?"

" Yes."

" Good. It is all up to Stellman."

" And the Sleeper."

" And the Sleeper," the old man nodded agreement at the young man's correction, " he is helping Stellman to the full?"

" Reports suggest he is."

" Good, good."

" Why . . .?" The thin man started to speak then stopped.

" What?" The thin man cleared his throat nervously.

" I am not questioning. I simply do not understand. Why use the Sleeper on this? It seems, well it seems . . ."

" Crude?"

" No I . . ."

" Yes crude is the word we used. It was a risk. It still is. He has been there for thirty years and it is a risk using him in this but we have to be certain. That is more important, much more important."

" I don't understand why you have never used him before."

" Think. Think. We have always used him. Everything he has done over the years has been for us. Every thought he has had, every decision he has made, every word he has spoken or written has been for us. Not overtly but gently, persuasively, over the years he has turned his position to our advantage. Sometimes consciously but mostly unconsciously he has worked for us. That is why we have never before used him for a specific task. He has been too useful for us. But now, this time we have had to use him. We had to take the risk."

" The risk of exposure?"

" No. There is no risk of that. No the risk was that he would not do it. Even he, probably, does not realise how useful he has been over the years. Invaluable would be a better word. He probably resents the fact that we are using him specifically for the first time in thirty years on something as crudely basic as this. That was the risk. It seems to be working."

" And afterwards?"

" Afterwards when he sees what we have planned he will understand and then all will be well and he will continue as before."

" For how long?"

" For how long? For ever. He will never come home. How could he?" The three men sat in silence for a moment before the young man stood and gathered up his papers.

" The next meeting is in two months time?"

" Yes, unless there is an emergency." The two men left and the old man pressed the button that reversed the wheelchair across the floor. He spun it so that he again faced the window. He waited for the car tail-lights to appear and sat until they had vanished down the road towards the city. Then he pressed a button on the wall and let the electric motor close the curtains. Then for a while he slept.

*　　*　　*

In London the Sleeper had been thinking thoughts that were astonishingly parallel to the conversation taking place thousands of miles away. And for the first time since the instructions had been received he began to understand the reason behind his thirty years of uncalled readiness. He had always been called. He had always been working for his masters. Everything he had done over the years of his exile had been slanted towards the benefit of his own country.

154

He wondered at his own lack of awareness that had led him to think he was merely awaiting a call to do a single job. Or was it a lack of awareness? Perhaps he had always known but he had thrust the knowledge deep into his subconscious and with it another thought that was in itself deeply disturbing.

*   *   *

He brought his mind back to the present with an effort. He had talked earlier that day to Stellman. The telephone call had been long and explicit. He had been able to assure the man that the plan was still set and that he had been able to bring pressure to bear that would ensure that the lead car would go the way Stellman wanted it to go on the Tuesday morning. Now he had done his part. Now it was all up to Stellman.

EIGHT

Stellman had spent most of Sunday and Monday in his hotel room. The waiting was becoming unbearable and he wanted to go out and drive using the car as he often used cars to release the stomach-gripping tension. But he did not. After the bombing he knew the police activity would be intense. He could not risk being stopped even on a routine enquiry. But he did go out twice on foot on the Sunday morning. The first time to buy several newspapers and the second time, after he had realised the papers told him nothing, to telephone the Sleeper. It was an unscheduled call but it was necessary. He had to know exactly what had happened and how the event would affect his own plans. The answers to his two questions were both settling and unsettling. It was settling to know that the plans for the meetings were unchanged even though he knew there would be a stepping-up in the security measures. It was unsettling to know that what the newspapers could only hint at was true. The bomb had been aimed at the President or the Prime Minister and it had been a very near miss.

On the Monday morning he had to go out. He drove a short distance into the country and lifted the motor-cycle from the boot of the Cortina. He spent about twenty minutes familiarising himself with the machine. It was an identical model to one he used on the island and he soon made the necessary adjustments to that particular machine's idiosyncracies. Then he returned to the hotel and tried to sleep.

*   *   *

Tuesday morning was a perfect English summer's day. The sky was a bright light blue when Stellman left the hotel near Reading and drove the Cortina towards London. At exactly eight o'clock he parked the car on a meter in Ennismore Street and put in enough coins to give him the two hour maximum period the meter allowed. He would be back before ten and he could not afford to have the car booked by a zealous Traffic Warden. There were few people about at eight o'clock. Most of the regular users of the parking spaces in the area were connected in some way with Imperial College and would not be there for another hour. And the tourists who would be visiting the nearby Museums were still breakfasting in their hotels.

*   *   *

He had dressed carefully that morning. The Walther rested under his left arm next to his skin. A flowery, brightly coloured shirt hung loose showing no sign of the automatic. His jacket was also loose and its plain dark grey contrasted oddly with the shirt, he wore a summer-weight trilby hat and sunglasses. He had hung a leather cased camera around his neck to complete the picture he wanted to project.

*   *   *

The second gun was in his suitcase and all the other items he had bought during his shopping expeditions were in a brown cardboard box. He was not going back to the hotel. From now until he left the country, the Cortina was his home.

*   *   *

He removed the motor-cycle from the boot and put all the other items in there before carefully closing the boot lid. He climbed onto the motor-cycle and set off towards the city centre. He rode steadily, winding among the dense early morning traffic on Kensington Road and Knightsbridge. The traffic thinned out a little when he turned into Constitution Hill and there was even less along The Mall. When he reached Trafalgar Square he pulled over to the pavement and climbing off he walked the machine towards the end of Pall Mall. There he stopped and propped the machine on its footrest and took off his jacket clipping it to the tray behind the saddle. The camera and the bright shirt gave him the appearance he wanted to evoke. Just another tourist. He stood relaxing the tense muscles in his neck and shoulders. With all the fussy care a bright-shirted tourist should take, he took one or two photographs. He waited. He glanced at his watch. It was almost nine and at that instant over the traffic noise he heard the chiming of the hour.

*   *   *

He closed up the camera and climbed onto the motor-cycle. He started the engine and pushed forward off the stand. He checked his watch. Three minutes past nine. He started moving slowly down Pall Mall. He looked at his watch again. He was too early. He turned right and made a circuit of St. James's Square and then came back onto Pall Mall. He turned left into Marlborough Road and then right onto The Mall. His timing was perfect. The lead car had already passed the memorial in front of Buckingham Palace and was signalling its left turn into Stable Yard Road.

*   *   *

Stellman accelerated the motor-cycle and cut in between the President's car and the back-up vehicle. He heard shouts from the men in the back-up car as he slid the cycle into the narrow nearside gap the President's car was leaving. The car was already slowing up for the turn into Cleveland Row where it would stop to discharge its passengers.

*   *   *

In the back-up car there was the confusion Stellman had expected. A camera-carrying tourist was what he looked like and what instinctively the security men had taken him for.

*   *   *

In the lead car Harry Walters looked back as they went round the corner. In that instant he saw the man on the motor-cycle. Like the other men his first reaction was that the man was a tourist inadvertently caught up in the procession of cars. Then his eyes left the bright shirt and the camera and concentrated on what he could see of the face. Then his car finished the turn and he lost sight of the man but in that same instant he knew who the man on the motor-cycle was.

*   *   *

Unfortunately Harry Walters made the wrong decision. He yelled to the driver to stop and started to open the door of the car. The driver obeyed his orders and behind him the driver of the Presidential limousine stopped too. Just as Stellman reached out a hand towards the door handle. The door opened, hinged at the back and Stellman looked into the face of the President of the United States of America from a range of less than six feet.

*   *   *

David Leeson was sitting in the far corner of the car and he stared in horrified amazement at the open door and the man sitting there on a motor-cycle. Leeson saw the shirt and the camera and thought for an incredulous instant that the man was a tourist there to wish him well and ask permission to take a photograph. Then the instant passed and with horrified fascination he saw the man's hand disappear to reappear a moment later holding a gun. The President heard only the first of the two shots that were fired.

*   *   *

Ahead of the President's car Walters was out of the lead car and had started back. He heard the two shots and hurled himself forward. The man on the motor-cycle started towards him and Walters gathered himself for the impact. Then Stellman fired again and Walters felt himself lifted

159

backwards to cannon against one of the security men who was following up from the lead car. Before he lost consciousness Walters was dimly aware of the shouts and cries and of the sound of the motor-cycle first loud and then diminishing as the rider accelerated away from the chaos he had left behind him.

*　　*　　*

The driver of the lead car reacted quickly as the shots echoed from the walls of the junction of the narrow streets. He had started to move forward again to let the cars behind him move and he was already picking up speed when the motorcyclist went past him. He accelerated away in pursuit. With the exception of the Englishman in the front passenger seat all the security guards were left standing at the scene of the shooting. The driver realised that too late and decided to press on. He glanced out of his eye corner at the man sitting beside him and caught a fleeting impression of shock and horror and something else.

*　　*　　*

The Englishman was reacting partly to the reality of what had happened and partly to the growing realisation that somehow he had been involved, not just in the scene of a few seconds ago, but in the lead up to that scene. He knew now that the orders he had followed when he gave the driver the route for that morning had been part of a plot. A plot which, if the man who had given him his orders was involved, had to be one of appalling magnitude. Beside him he saw the driver reach for the radiomicrophone to call in to headquarters. He concentrated on the motor-cyclist who was now turning to the right. That was the first objective. The man had to be caught. Alive.

160

*　　*　　*

Lewis Comoy had been persuaded to rest. He knew he needed
to rest and he knew he was likely to make errors of judgement if he did not. He sat in the colonel's office trying to
relax. He sat up with a start as the door burst open and Hunt
yelled at him.

" There's been a shooting. Someone has shot the President."

" Jesus." Comoy's tiredness disappeared and he sprinted
after Hunt as the Colonel ran down the corridor leading to
the rear entrance to the Embassy. A car was already waiting,
doors open, for them and the driver hit the accelerator before
either of the two men were in their seats. The doors were
slammed shut by the speed of the start and it was several
seconds before they had untangled themselves sufficiently for
Comoy to start asking questions.

" What happened?"

" We're not sure. What we do know is that someone shot
the President at close range while he was still in the car."

" Where?"

" Outside the Conference centre."

" Nothing else?"

" Only garbled stuff. The gunman was on a motor-cycle
and one of the escort cars is after him. We got all this from
the back-up car." Hunt leaned forward and spoke urgently
into the microphone of the car radio. The speaker crackled
slightly before the central operator's voice came out strongly
and calmly.

" Subject travelling east along Pall Mall. Lead car in
pursuit, driver and one guard on board. We have one message from the driver saying subject had turned into Waterloo
Place then nothing."

" What about the President?"

" He has been taken to the medical room in the Confer-

161

ence Centre."

Comoy grabbed the microphone from the Colonel's hand.

" Why there? Get him to a hospital."

" Agent-in-charge has command of situation sir." Comoy sat back with an exclamation. He looked out of the window. The driver had the siren on and the car was already on Constitution Hill and the speed was increasing. The driver went round the flat curve into The Mall the tyres screeching a warning to the pedestrians who were already looking to the east trying to identify the many sirens and alarms that were sounding. The driver braked hard for the turn into Stable Yard Road and came to a stop almost at once. Comoy and Hunt scrambled out and ran past the stationary back-up car and the Presidential car. One of the small group of men standing near the President's car waved them by and they went round the corner into Cleveland Row and past the guards gathered at the doors of the Conference Centre. They recognised Comoy and the Colonel instantly and the two men hurried through the doors.

" Who's in charge?" Comoy asked the Colonel.

" Draycott."

" Where's Draycott?" Comoy snapped at one of the men he recognised from the Embassy permanent detail.

" First floor back, sir, medical room." The two men took the staircase two steps at a time and followed the line of guards to the door of the medical room. Comoy pushed open the door. A man in a white coat of a doctor looked up briefly and then continued drawing a blanket over the head of a body lying on the table in the centre of the room.

*   *   *

The driver of the lead car had followed Stellman into Waterloo Place. Before he made the turn he had managed to announce the move to the radio operator, then as he straightened up he realised he had gained on the motor cyclist. So much so that he was within a few feet of the machine's rear wheel. He had barely time to record that the fleeing gunman was stopping when the motor-cycle made a sudden u-turn. The driver's instinctive reaction was to brake hard. In so doing he presented Stellman with a head-on, almost stationary target. Beside him the driver heard the English guard curse softly and start to raise his gun but it was too late. From that range Stellman could not miss and he didn't.

Stellman flung the motor-cycle round again and continued on the way he had been going. He mounted the pavement and rode the machine to the head of a long flight of steps. He did not slow down and went bouncing noisily down the steps scattering pedestrians in all directions. He hit the pavement at the foot of the steps and shot across The Mall into the road that bounded the east end of the park.

When he turned into the traffic approaching Parliament Square he was beginning to tense again. Everything had gone well. He had only a short distance to go and then he would be clear. He crossed Westminster Bridge and went round the roundabout before turning left into the cluster of narrow streets opposite the hospital. Both sides of all those small streets were lined with parked vehicles and he stopped underneath one of the overhead railway bridges and turned off the engine. He untied the grey jacket from the tray behind the saddle of the motor-cycle and slipped it on over the bright shirt.

He pushed his hat into one of the jacket pockets then he lifted the machine into a space between two cars standing its nose into the kerb. He locked the front wheel and then walked slowly back cutting through a little park where a small army of holidaying children were noisily playing on the few swings and climbing frames. He stopped near a litter basket and watched them. When he was sure no one was watching him he dropped the camera into the basket and walked on.

He recrossed Westminster Bridge walking slowly. Once over the bridge he went down into the Underground station and was grateful for the feeling of security it gave him. Twenty minutes later he came up at South Kensington station and walked down Exhibition Road back to where he had left the Cortina. He opened the boot and took out his suitcase. He climbed into the driving seat and making sure he was unobserved he slipped out of his jacket and pulled a plain cream shirt over the coloured one and then pulled the grey jacket over the top. He glanced at his watch. It was ten-fifteen, he was out in his estimate.

He started the car and drove steadily west eventually crossing the river on Hammersmith Bridge. By the time he reached the place where he had left the motor-cycle the tension caused by the reaction to the job had begun to ease. There was no one about and in the darkness created by the railway bridge over the road he took off the coloured shirt and folded it up into a small bundle. He removed the holster containing the Walther and replaced it with the Beretta although this time he wore the holster over the cream shirt. That done he unlocked the motor-cycle and put it into the boot of the Cortina. Finally he took the folded shirt wrapped the hat and the Walther in it and pushed it under his seat. He drove slowly around the mean streets until he found a parking space. He locked the Cortina and headed for Lambeth North Underground station. Half an hour later he was in Sloane Square and strolling with the shoppers and tourists enjoying the warm sunshine along Kings Road. It was almost noon when he turned into Flood Street.

*   *   *

In the medical room at the Conference Centre Comoy had stopped as if transfixed by the sight that had met his eyes. Hunt towered over him and Comoy heard the hiss as the Colonel drew in his breath. "Mr. Comoy." Comoy turned his head slowly and looked at the man who had spoken. It was Draycott the agent-in-charge of the day's security detail. Comoy opened his mouth to speak then closed it again. Over his shoulder he heard Hunt's voice.

"What happened for Christ's sake." The doctor looked up from the body on the table.

"Not here. Go somewhere else." Comoy nodded and turned and followed the Colonel into the corridor. Draycott followed them and then brushed past to lead the way into a small cramped office. The three men crowded in.

"Well?"

"We had no chance. No chance at all."

"For Christ's sake. What do you mean no chance? Every man here was a highly trained security officer. Trained to protect life. To protect one life. And everyone of you have screwed it up."

"But . . ."

"There are no buts Goddammit. The man in there is the President. Was the President. Two assassination attempts in four days and we lose him at the second attempt. Dear God the defence should have been impregnable."

"But Mr. Comoy," Draycott at last broke in, "the President isn't dead." The silence that fell in the small room was almost tangible as for a long moment Comoy stared into Draycott's eyes.

"What did you say?"

"That wasn't the President sir. The President is hurt but he isn't dead."

"Then who . . .?"

"That was Creighton, one of the guards. Inspector Walters the Englishman was shot too but he's alive."

165

" Then where the hell is he? The President."

" He's here sir. On the next floor. There is another medical room there. We . . ." Draycott found himself talking to an empty room as Comoy and the Colonel pushed their way to the door and ran for the stairs.

*　　*　　*

The second doctor was obviously aware of his responsibilities but he had the calm air that came as part of the experience of doing his job.

" No you can't see him. He is conscious, just, and he is in shock. He is also receiving blood. Don't worry gentlemen, Mr. Leeson will live."

" Hospital?" Comoy found it difficult to speak coherently for a moment. " Shouldn't he . . .?"

" Not for the moment. The unit here is the best there can be. We have everything that is needed. Later we will consider moving the President but for now he is as well here as he would be anywhere else. Medically speaking that is. I expect you will find it easier to make this place secure than a public hospital so perhaps he is safer here than in hospital." Comoy nodded at the doctor and backed slowly out of the room. He became aware that his head was hurting again. He brushed his hand across his eyes and gestured to the Colonel to follow him as he went back down the stairs. Halfway down Comoy stopped.

" Frank, check the measures Draycott has taken then meet me downstairs. I want to talk to Adams." Hunt turned and went back up the stairs in search of the agent-in-charge and Comoy found a small room with a telephone on the first floor close to the room where Creighton's body lay. He was through to the Commissioner in moments.

" What do you know?"

" Nothing Mr. Comoy. All we have is the report of a

166

shooting then your people clamped down."

"Right. There was a shooting. The President has been shot, the doctor says he will be okay. I'm afraid your man Walters was hurt too. The assass . . . the gunman was riding a motor-cycle for God's sake and one of our men is after him . . . wait." The door opened and Colonel Hunt pushed into the room.

"Lewis, the driver of the lead car, he went after the man on the motor-cycle, he's dead and so is the guard who was with him. The gunman rode down the steps, what are they called, the Duke of Wellington steps. Eyewitnesses said he went across the park. After that nothing."

"Description?"

"Not much. It seems Walters was the only one that got a good look at him and probably the two men he shot in Waterloo Place. He was wearing a hat, a bright coloured floral pattern shirt, everyone agrees that, and he had something hung round his neck. Might have been a camera or it might have been the holster for the weapon." Comoy turned to the telephone again.

"Commissioner . . . assume it's the man from the motel, wearing a bright coloured shirt looking like a tourist. Do what you can." He replaced the telephone and looked up at the Colonel. "We've lost him Frank."

"Not necessarily . . ."

"We've lost him. The motor-bike, the shirt, the camera, all part of the blind. By now he will have ditched the lot. He used the bike to let him get in and out quickly where a car or being on foot would not have worked. The shirt was to make people look and see that and not see his face. The camera part of the dressing. Just another tourist. By now he will be dressed in a suit and be in a car or on a train or any damned thing. We've lost him and we might as well accept it and not waste time and effort on it. Let's concentrate on stopping a repeat performance."

" A repeat?"

" He missed didn't he? When he finds that out he will be back. The bombing didn't put him off and neither will anything else. He will try again." He stood up and suddenly looked years older than he had before. " Christ, I can't believe it. We knew he was here and we were still caught. The guy has a charmed life." He made a conscious effort and straightened himself, " where are we controlling this from?"

" Draycott has a radio van outside."

" Let's go." The two men went out into the street where a radio control van was drawn up at the kerb. Inside two radio operators in headphones were bent over sets. Draycott looked up as the Colonel and Comoy walked in.

" What have we got? From the beginning."

" The man was travelling down The Mall in the opposite direction to the motorcade. One of the men noticed him but took him to be a tourist. The way he was dressed and . . ."

" Yes . . . go on."

" He made the turn into Stable Yard Road and went in between the President's car and the back-up car. The back-up crew still thought he was a sightseer caught up by chance. Walters, the English policeman was in the lead car. Apparently he looked round and suddenly yelled to stop and the driver did so. We don't know why he yelled but a guess is that he recognised the man on the motor-cycle or simply had a sixth sense reaction who he was. The driver probably stopped out of reflex action to an order. Anyway he stopped just round the bend in the road and that meant the President's car had to stop as well. It couldn't get round and it couldn't back up. I . . . I was in the car with the President. I didn't know anything until the lead car stopped. Before I knew what was going on the door was opened . . ."

" What?"

" He opened the door of the car."

" Jesus Christ."

"He opened the door and fired two shots at the President. Then he went off on his motor-cycle. I opened my door and was climbing out to try to get a shot at him when I heard another two shots. That was when he killed Creighton and wounded Walters. I yelled to MacKinley to take charge of the President and I started after the bike on foot. Then the lead car went off after him. By that time all but one of the guards in the lead car were out on the roadway. We found the remaining guard and the driver dead in the car in Waterloo Place both shot through the head. According to eyewitnesses the gunman then rode his machine down the steps and disappeared along the road that runs across the back of Horse Guards Parade." Comoy nodded slowly.

"Okay. Frank, let's talk." Comoy went down the steps from the radio van onto the pavement and stood for a moment hesitantly then he walked over to one of the cars drawn up outside the Conference Centre and pulled open the door. He climbed into the back seat and the Colonel followed him.

"I take it the other delegates have been warned off?"

"Yes."

"Right. Let's look at what we have. The gunman arrived on the scene at exactly the right moment. He wasn't standing waiting for the car to arrive. He rode up exactly at the right moment and in exactly the right place."

"So . . ."

"So he knew where and he knew when. He has someone inside our security operation."

"Okay Lewis, you're guessing but I agree it seems a likely explanation. Where do we start?"

"God knows." Comoy ran his hand over his face in a gesture combining tiredness and frustration. "There is another thing. Why did he kill the driver and the guard in the car that went after him?"

"What do you mean why? They were after him."

169

"Yes I know. But look, the gunman turned into Waterloo Place right, then he went down those steps. They couldn't have followed him in the car. If they had got out of the car and gone on foot they would have lost him. So why bother to kill them? We're not dealing with a crazy man who shoots people for kicks. He shot the driver and the guard because they were a danger to him. One or the other or both of them must have been in on it."

"The guard was one of the four with authority to select the route."

"Okay, check with Draycott. My bet is that the Englishman was the one who selected today's route." The colonel climbed out of the car and went back to the radio van. He was back within seconds and slid in behind Comoy.

"You win your bet."

"He picked the route?"

"Yes."

"Then that is why he was killed and the driver probably got it because he had seen our man from too close range." Comoy broke off as a guard came down the steps and walked over to the car.

"Good news of the President sir. He is fully conscious and talking. He wants to see you Mr. Comoy."

"Right. I'll be in at once." Comoy climbed out of the car followed by the colonel. The two men went into the building and up the stairs. Comoy walked over to the door that led to the room where the President lay. He looked back at Hunt.

"Frank."

"Yes, I'll start digging."

"Good." Comoy looked at the door, his expression a clear indication that he was not expecting to enjoy the next few minutes.

NINE

Janet Ainsley and John Perring had heard nothing of the attack on the President. They had done as they had planned for that Tuesday morning. Janet had announced the need for some urgent shopping hinting vaguely that it concerned the many functions she would be attending over the course of the coming week. Perring had automatically accompanied her and they were on their way to his flat in Flood Street before nine o'clock. There, Perring had hesitated only briefly before deciding to leave the telephone on its hook. Anyone in official quarters would know he was out with the Foreign Secretary's wife and would be unlikely to try to call him. If someone did an engaged signal would be suspicious. The second telephone he had to leave. He did not expect Stellman to make contact but he could not risk cutting off the line of communication.

* * *

He spent some time in the kitchen making coffee conscious that he was gaining less pleasure from the stolen time together than he should. He knew the reason lay in the gathering tension as time passed without Stellman making his move. He knew it had to be almost any day. The conference had only five more days to run. There was another reason. During the time spent away from her he was able to assess his relationship with Janet Ainsley more objectively. He had accepted, however unwillingly, that he was in love with her but the enormity of attempting to do anything about that love was too great.

Apart from the scandal of revealing to her husband what was happening there was the danger to him when his masters found out. They would eliminate him. And there would be nowhere for him to hide. They would find him, or rather someone would. Not Stellman, he was not worth that but someone in the same line of business although lower in the scale. He wondered to himself if there was a way he could terminate the affair without hurting her. That was again a new experience for him, thinking of someone else first.

" What are you thinking about?" Janet Ainsley had come into the tiny kitchen and he was startled out of his thoughts.

" Oh. Sorry, thinking about work. There is so much going on at the moment. Sorry Janet. I'll stop. The coffee is almost ready. Go back into the living room. I'll bring it." As she turned away he saw the tiny frown lines that caught at her forehead and he felt the sudden, only recently familiar, lurch inside.

*   *   *

When he went through into the other room it was empty. He glanced at the outer door but the safety chain was still in place. He went to the bedroom. The curtains were drawn and Janet was already in bed her clothes folded neatly on a chair by the window. Perring put the tray he was carrying carefully on the side table. He sat on the edge of the bed and looked at her. She was not smiling and her expression was grave.

" You're changing your mind, aren't you?"

" No, no it isn't that. I love you Janet, I do, it's just that . . ."

" Stop. Don't say anything more. Let's go on as we were. At least for now. Later, later we can talk again. When we have both had time to think." He seized gratefully at the opportunity to postpone the problem. It would be no better later, he knew, but at least Stellman would be finished and he would know what his masters wanted him to do next. That might make the decision easier to reach. He drew back the cover and looked with rising excitement at her body. He leaned forward and very gently began to stroke and kiss her. Soon she was responding, twisting and turning on the bed and moaning softly her eyes closed as if to shut out the unpleasantness that had been temporarily averted. Perring undressed rapidly and pulled the covers completely away and lay down beside her. She turned towards him and swiftly, urgently they began to make love.

*   *   *

Later they made love again. This time slowly and gently and lovingly. He felt her drawing everything she could from their coupling as if she thought it would be their last. They were lying half sleeping in each other's arms when the doorbell jarred them both into alarmed wakefulness.

*   *   *

Perring waited for several moments before going to the wall 'phone by the outer door. Just as he had decided not to answer the ordinary telephone had it rung he was unwilling to answer the door bell. He waited and the bell rang again. He lifted the intercom handset carefully.
" Yes."
" Perring. I want to see you." There was no mistaking the quiet voice. It was Stellman. Like a man in a dream Perring pressed the lock release button to open the street door.

*   *   *

In the few minutes it took Stellman to climb the stairs Perring had hurried through to the bedroom. He told Janet there was someone coming up to talk. The business was urgent and could not wait and she would have to remain where she was and she had to keep quiet. He pulled a towelling robe on and had just time to slip off the safety chain when he heard Stellman arrive at the door.

* * *

Opening the door he had the first sudden feeling of alarm for after taking great care to avoid being seen Stellman was suddenly there in broad daylight, all caution apparently forgotten. The feeling of alarm faded rapidly when he saw the man in the corridor. Slightly built and of medium height he looked anything other than dangerous and like many men before him Perring lowered his guard. He opened the door wider and Stellman came into the room.

" Sit down. Do you want a drink?" Stellman sat down and shook his head. Perring felt slightly foolish dressed as he was and he half turned as if to go into the bedroom to change and then turned back knowing he could not risk opening the door.

" What do you want?"

" I want you to make contact with the man you have waiting."

" Now?"

" Yes."

" Then you're ready to do the job?" Stellman looked at Perring carefully. There was no doubt about it. The man had no idea what had happened that morning.

" Yes," he answered.

" Still planning to meet at the Marquis of Granby?"

" Yes."

" When?"

" Today. Six o'clock. Exactly." Perring reached for the

telephone and then remembered he did not want an engaged signal on that line and instead he opened a cupboard door and took out the unlisted instrument. Stellman watched him interestedly and waited as Perring dialled a number.

"It's me. The job at the Marquis. Today. Six o'clock sharp. Right." He replaced the receiver and looked at Stellman with a smile. "All okay." Stellman nodded.

"Your day off?" The sudden change of direction made Perring start.

"Er. Yes."

"I thought from the schedule you gave me you were on duty today?"

"Er, no, or rather I was but they changed the shifts."

"Oh. Catching up on lost sleep?"

"Yes." Stellman stood up his movement fluid and controlled. Perring started to follow suit then stopped to fall back into the cushions on the chair as he saw the heavy ended, silenced automatic pointing at him. His eyes darted to the bedroom door and back again. The movement was swift but it did not escape Stellman.

"Do not speak," he said softly, "just nod or shake your head. Is there anyone in there?" Perring shook his head, sweat already breaking out on his forehead. Stellman shook his head gently as if in sorrow. Then he leaned forward as if to speak confidentially to the man in the armchair. The movement was easy and natural and Perring was hardly aware that the movement had also brought the automatic closer until he felt the gentle touch of the silencer against his temple. In one fleeting instant of time he knew what was about to happen but that instant was too short for him to do anything. He had no time to move or to speak or to pray. Stellman squeezed the trigger and Perring died.

*　　*　　*

175

In the bedroom Janet Ainsley had accepted the hastily concocted tale Perring had told her and she lay warm and relaxed under the covers. Deep down she knew the affair was doomed to a short life. At first she had hoped that it would be another story but she was too intelligent to believe that Perring was the kind of man who would go through the inevitable circus that would surround them when, if, she left her husband. With an acceptance that was almost cold-blooded she had decided in the few days since they had last been together, that she would get from their relationship all she could in whatever time they had left together. At least she would have memories to keep. She remembered the love-making that had just ended and the memory began to arouse her and she grew impatient waiting for Perring to finish the business he had outside.

*   *   *

The noise from the living room startled but did not alarm her. She lay for a moment trying to decide what it had been and then the door opened. The sunlight that filled the outer room threw into silhouette the figure of a man that stood there looking into the shaded bedroom. She sat up in alarm. She knew instantly it wasn't Perring, the man was several inches shorter. He stepped forward quickly and silently and Janet Ainsley saw the gun in his hand. Her mouth opened to scream but the man had reached the bed and her scream was stopped as the noise she had heard came again and in the incalculable moment of time before she died she knew that Perring too was dead.

*   *   *

For Comoy the day that had begun like a nightmare had barely improved. Out of the entire shambles only the fact that the President was not dead stood out as a plus. Everything else was a minus. The few minutes he had spent with the President before the doctor abruptly put an end to the meeting had been as bitter as anything he could have imagined. The President was hurt physically, mentally he was frightened and angry and the anger was not reserved solely for the gunman.

"Incompetence. Sheer incompetence. You have no right to be in charge of a Summer Camp let alone a security operation. For God's sake Comoy what are your people playing at? Do they want me dead? Are your own people behind it? On Saturday the bomb. Today this. Goddam it man. To let that man ride up and open . . . open the car door and . . ." The President spluttered to a stop his voice finishing on a high querulous note. He glared at Comoy and was silent for a moment. When he started to speak again he had regained control and there was a venomous undercurrent to his spoken words.

"What is behind it Comoy? And who? This wasn't the work of an amateur although God knows an amateur could have got through the defence you gave me. It isn't the Russians and I don't think it's the Chinese. Who does that leave? One of the smaller nations? Like Israel perhaps?" Comoy felt his face begin to darken but he said nothing. "The Israelis have had it in for me," the President went on, "ever since I stopped aid and the atomic power plants Nixon promised them. Was it them? If it was you would be their logical contact wouldn't you? Did they get to you Comoy? Are you working for them?" Comoy looked into the protuberant eyes and for a moment the two men glared at each other in silence and then the President must have seen something of the depth of hatred the security man had for him as for the first time since the beginning of his tirade a hint of alarm showed. Then the President looked away.

"Mr. President," Comoy began when he was sure he

177

could speak without his feelings showing in his voice, " you have been hurt and you are in pain and probably in shock too. When you feel better you will know what you have just said is nonsense. Not just about me but about Israel as well. You have every right to be critical of me, it was my job to prevent this kind of thing and I've failed and you are entitled to expect my resignation and if you want it you can have it. But right now, for better or worse, I'm the best man you have. Think about it, you know my record and you know that I serve the President regardless of who he is."

" Alright Comoy. Get on with it. But I am not refusing to accept your resignation. When I get back to the States we will take up that matter again."

" Yes sir." Comoy was grateful for the implied truce. He had not changed his opinion of the man but he had a job to do.

" Now, the man who shot you, can you describe him?"

" What is there to describe? He looked like anyone. A hat, dark glasses, a bright shirt. Nothing else I remember."

" Thank you sir. I have to go now I will keep you informed."

" Tell me when you have him. I'm not interested in the details. And Comoy, I haven't entirely bought your claim that Israel isn't behind this. I know that you would say that. You people stick together." That was when the doctor had gently but firmly steered Comoy to the door and he had not resisted, he was pleased to get away. At the door the President's voice stopped him. The tone had changed. It was soft and bitter and he meant every word.

" I want heads Comoy. Yours or others." Comoy had nodded without turning his head and then the door closed behind him.

*   *   *

The guards outside the door had studiously looked the other way as he leaned against the door for a moment. Then he went in search of Colonel Hunt. The colonel was in the middle of a seething mass of men and papers and there was an air of resigned acceptance that a major error had been made and that they were all being made to look foolish and incompetent. Comoy walked over and stood beside the colonel.

" Anything?"

" Nothing Lewis. Dead ends. I can't find anything to tie either the Englishman, Matthews or the driver in. Nothing at all. But we're still digging."

" What about Adams. Has he got anything for us?"

" Not so far. They have picked up a few hundred motor-cyclists but I reckon that's a waste of time."

" So do I. Our man has ditched that by now. Well what next? We've had two attempts in the past four days, both of them too damned close for comfort, I don't have a lot of faith in our ability to stand another attempt."

" You reckon there will be another try?"

" The President is still alive isn't he?"

" And by now our man will know it. The tv people have got most of it. And what they haven't got they can guess. They're having a field day out there."

" What are these?" Comoy indicated a pile of pink files, some slim some bulky, on the desk top.

" Preliminary reports, medicals, ballistics so on. The detailed reports will come later." Comoy sat down and began to turn the pages rapidly his eyes raking down and pausing only when something caught his eye.

" That's odd."

" What is?"

" I hadn't thought about it before. Too many damned things happening at once."

" What?"

179

" The President was hit twice. Once on the thigh and once in the upper arm. Both flesh wounds, both left hand side which is what you would expect since the gunman opened the nearside door. Ballistics say the bullets were nine milli- metre copper jacketed. Same in the three dead men and the one they dug out of Walters. They haven't done a check yet but we can assume that all six bullets came from the same gun."

" Well?"

" How far was he from Walters and Creighton when he shot them?"

" About ten feet."

" And from the car when he shot the other two?"

" Uncertain, eyewitness reports were poor."

" Still we can guess. He fired from ahead because the bullets went through the windscreen so it must have been at least the same distance."

" Go on."

" Four shots at a range of ten feet or more. All when he was riding a motor-cycle, presumably one-handed and at least one when the target was moving and alert. What does that tell you?"

" That he's a good man with a gun. We expect that."

" Then why didn't he kill the President? Two shots at a sitting target and he was stationary too and he was at a range of what, five feet, six feet at the most. Christ Almighty Frank he couldn't have missed. Not him. Not at that range."

Hunt stared at Comoy for almost a minute as the two men sat in silence.

" What are you driving at Frank? You don't think . . .?"

" I don't know what I think. But I do know our boy is up to something. No let up Frank. We want total alertness on this from now on. I want the net around the President so tight Jesus Christ himself couldn't get through." The tele- phone rang and Comoy reached for it. " Hello. Oh, hello

180

Commissioner. No, nothing more. How about you? No, well keep trying. Wait, Commissioner, what are you doing about ports and airports? Good." He replaced the telephone and glanced at the colonel. "Nothing, but he's closing the net. Our man will have a hard time getting out."

*　　*　　*

Stellman had worked quickly and efficiently after the shootings. He stripped off the holster that had held the Beretta and stowed it away in a drawer in Perring's bedroom. Then he removed the silencer from the barrel of the automatic and slipped it into his pocket.

He folded the dead man's fingers around the black plastic handgrip of the gun and held the arm up so that the gun pointed at the wound in the temple. Then he let the arm fall away, the gun dropping into the chair by Perring's side. It teetered momentarily then tipped over and dropped to the floor. Carefully he looked round the room. Everything appeared normal. The unlisted telephone would cause the security officers some thought but that could not be helped. It might, he thought, be necessary for some covering up to be done.

He went swiftly and quietly down the stairs and out into the street. He walked back towards the underground station. On the way he bought a blue air letter and wrote a terse note before addressing it and dropping it into a post box. The tidying up of Perring's trail would be started within hours. It should be soon enough. If it wasn't it would not be any concern of his. They should have chosen their help more carefully.

*　　*　　*

He took a very long ride on the tube train. Riding round and

181

round, changing trains occasionally so as not to draw attention to himself. It was a harmless and safe way of passing the time. When he eventually came up into the streets, once more at Lambeth North station, he was ready for the next stage and already growing impatient. He quelled the impatience carefully. He turned the Cortina west and drove steadily out towards the Kingston By-Pass and the Marquis of Granby.

*　　*　　*

The man Perring had telephoned in the last act he was to do in his life, was exactly on time. The car park at the pub was almost empty at six o'clock. Stellman walked over to the car, a grey Jaguar several years old, and leaned in at the window.

" Mr. Kwok?"

" Yes." The driver of the Jaguar was about thirty five years old. He looked and was a hard man. His face carried scars that showed he had not had a gentle life. He had lived in England most of his life and he rarely spoke Chinese anymore. His accent was almost gone.

" My friend told you what to do?"

" Yes. You have two parcels for me. One I ditch where it won't be found. Ever. The other I keep safe for you when you come back into the country next year."

" Right."

" And I get five hundred now. The same next year when I give you back the stuff."

" Right." Stellman walked back to the white Cortina and lifted the cardboard box from the boot. He motioned to the other man who climbed out and opened the boot of the Jaguar. Stellman gently placed the box on the floor of the boot. Kwok walked back to his seat and Stellman reached in to gently touch the box and then even more gently he closed the boot lid. He walked over to the Cortina and came back with a small brightly coloured bundle. He handed it to the man.

"Put that out of sight. In the glove box." He waited until it was done and then handed over an envelope. "That's your first five hundred. Listen. The box in the boot you lose. Forever. That," he pointed at the glove box, "you keep for me. Okay?" The man nodded. "Okay now you stay here for two minutes. Then get moving. Don't hang around here. Two minutes is all."

"Okay." Stellman walked back to the Cortina and started the engine. He drove out of the car park and glanced once at the man who was carefully counting the money Stellman had given him. Stellman turned the Cortina into the road signposted to Hampton Court. He drove about three hundred yards before stopping and switching off the engine. He wound down the window and waited.

*   *   *

In the Jaguar Ronald Kwok finished counting the money and glanced at his watch. He grinned, the job had sounded easy when Perring had approached him. Now it looked even easier. It was money for nothing. He started the engine. He glanced at his watch again. Two minutes the man had said. For five hundred cash in his hand he would be precise. He slipped the automatic into "drive" and moved forward.

*   *   *

In the cardboard box in the boot an inertia switch rocked backwards with the movement and made a contact.

*   *   *

Stellman heard the explosion quite clearly from where he sat. He wound up the window and started the engine. He drove steadily away from the area. After a few minutes a police car roared past him travelling towards the Marquis of Granby. A few minutes after that a fire engine followed the police car. Stellman leaned back in his seat and began to whistle softly to himself.

TEN

The round the clock watch on Perring that had been ordered had turned up nothing that interested the small man in the office on the top floor of the French Embassy. Then Janet Ainsley had arrived at the Flood Street flat and a relatively short time later another visitor had appeared. The man on duty had immediately called in and reported. He knew the Foreign Secretary's wife by sight and he was quick enough to know that he would be caught flat-footed if all three left the flat within a few minutes of one another. The small man thought for a moment after he had listened to the report.

"I will send another man to join you. You stay with Perring, he will cover the unknown man, at least until we know who he is. There is no need to keep a separate watch on the woman we can pick up her trail whenever we need to." He replaced the receiver and called his assistant. The man they sent to watch Stellman was the only one available for immediate duty. By nothing more than good luck he was their most able man in the difficult art of surveillance. The man was in place within minutes and when Stellman left the flat he never for one moment suspected that the one thing he had avoided so carefully since arriving in England had finally happened. He had acquired a tail.

*   *   *

Comoy arrived at the Commissioner's office within minutes of Adams' call.

"We've got something Mr. Comoy, although I'm not entirely certain what. Last night, a little after six o'clock there was an explosion in the car park at the Marquis of Granby, that's a pub on the A3 just outside Kingston, the explosion was in a car. There wasn't a lot left but what there was ties in with the attempt on the President. Other things are being checked but this is it so far. The car was a Jaguar registered in the name of Ronald Kwok, he's known to us, and the explosion seems to have been in the boot. There is very little left of whatever the bomb was made of so there are no leads there so far. However, on Kwok's body were the remains of money, about five hundred pounds as far as we can see. In the glove box, hardly damaged at all in the explosion or in the fire, was an automatic pistol wrapped in a brightly coloured floral shirt. The pistol is a Walther PPK nine millimetre with one bullet left in a seven bullet magazine. It's a leap to assume that means six shots were fired from it but in view of the shirt it's a leap that may be justified."

"Ballistics?"

"They have the gun now and are checking against the report on the bullets taken from the President's car and from the three dead men."

"The man in the car, Kwok you said, what nationality is he?"

"British. He came here from Hong Kong about twelve years ago and he has given us a lot of trouble since."

"You mean he's Chinese?"

"Technically he is a British subject but yes he is Chinese."

"Dear God that's all we want."

"What? Oh, you mean . . . yes I see. I hadn't thought of the political implications. That could cause some problems between you and the Chinese. But this man is from

Hong Kong not the mainland."

"That won't stop them Commissioner. The press and the t.v. boys. They'll make a connection whether one exists or not. It isn't going to do any good at all to relationships. I don't just mean this conference, that's going down the drain rapidly anyway. The President is not in a fit state to attend and even if he was he is in anything but a diplomatic frame of mind." Comoy paused and looked thoughtfully at the Commissioner. "Is there any chance of keeping this quiet. What do you call it? A D. notice?"

"No chance, anyway that would cover only our own people and there are journalists here from every country you can think of." The telephone rang and Adams reached out to pick up the instrument. He listened for several minutes his face growing darker. He replaced the telephone and looked at Comoy. "We're too late. It's already been on t.v. A claim of a direct link between the attempt on the President and an unnamed Chinaman."

"Christ. How did that happen?"

"I don't know but it's done. I take it that finishes the conference?"

"I think we can assume that. There was some friction between the French and the Chinese apparently but somehow your government smoothed it over but with the President shot and now this. Yes, you can reckon it's over." There was silence in the large room for a moment.

"We are cutting down the search for your man," the Commissioner said.

"Why?"

"Surely that's obvious?"

"You mean this man Kwok? He's a red herring Commissioner. He has to be. Until now we have had nothing to tie in a man of Oriental appearance. This is a set-up. It has to be."

"None of the descriptions tie in, I agree, but the only
186

three people who had a clear look at the gunman were Walters and your driver and Matthews and they are not in a position to tell us whether the man was an Oriental or not." Comoy nodded and held his head in his hands for a moment. Then he sat up and looked at the Commissioner. "Do you know what this reminds me of? Dallas in 1963. No I don't mean the police work although I will be the first to admit that our own security has left a lot to be desired. But all the rest. Leads, more leads, all apparently feasible and all confusing the main issue. I don't like any of it. I may have a suspicious mind but it seems to me that things are happening too rapidly. And too confusingly." The American stopped as the telephone rang again. Adams spoke into it and then listened, his face hardening. He stood up before the voice at the other end of the line had finished speaking.

"Problems?"

"Yes I'm afraid so. Nothing to do with this. There has been a double shooting, our men think it's a murder and suicide. You stay here, I'll see that the ballistics and any other reports are fed through to you."

"Commissioner why you, on a murder case, that's routine isn't it?"

"Normally yes, only this isn't normal. One of the dead is the wife of Michael Ainsley, the Foreign Secretary."

*   *   *

Charles Fox sat alone in the back of the car as it wound through the streets towards the Hill Street flat used by the Home Secretary. The message from Peter Evans had been garbled and the Prime Minister was worried. Worried enough to go himself. The car stopped and Fox climbed out, he glanced back and saw the ever present guard car draw up and two dark suited men followed him as he walked along the pavement. He went up the steps to the front door. It opened to his ring.

"Prime Minister, please come in sir." He knew the security man well.

"Good evening Harry, Mr. Evans in his study?"

"Yes sir."

"Good, I know the way." He strolled down the thickly carpeted corridor and opened the door to the study and went in. The Home Secretary was sitting in an upright chair by his wide desk. His eyes were open but even before he reached his side the Prime Minister knew he was dead. He stopped and looked at the face of a man whose last days had been lived in such torment. He felt no surprise. If anything there was a feeling of inevitability. He glanced at the desk top and saw the two envelopes. He picked them up and read the inscriptions. He carefully opened them both and read their short contents. Then he put one of the letters back on the desk. The other and the two torn envelopes he slipped into an inside pocket. "Poor Peter," he murmured. He walked back to the door and called for the security man.

*   *   *

When the Commissioner arrived at the Home Secretary's flat he was shown into the small sitting room where the Prime Minister waited.

"Commissioner. It's a sorry business."

"Yes sir. Seems to be no doubt that it was suicide."

"So I understand. I wonder . . ."

"Yes sir?"

"I was thinking aloud really Commissioner. The last few days I have had other things on my mind and I may not have been as cautious as I might otherwise have been. I was wondering if inadvertently I had said something that had made him realise we were investigating him."

188

"I don't know sir. Of course it may be that he had found out about the investigations himself. It would not be beyond possibility, after all he is, was, in overall charge of the police."

"True."

"Has his wife been told?"

"No, the doctors think she is still too weak. The daughter is a lot better but I have suggested they do not tell her yet, in the circumstances I thought it would be for the best."

"Yes I agree. Later perhaps when . . . well of course there will be no investigation now. It will be closed."

"Quite."

"There is something else sir."

"What?"

"Mrs. Ainsley."

"Janet Ainsley?"

"Yes."

"Why what has happened? She isn't in any trouble is she?"

"I'm afraid she is dead sir."

"Dead? Dear God. How?"

"She has been shot. Murdered."

"Mur . . ."

"I'm afraid so sir. She was at a flat in Flood Street, the flat is leased to one of the security men on the Foreign Secretary's staff. He was there too. Also dead. It looks like suicide for him but we're not sure yet."

"But I don't understand. What was Janet Ainsley doing there?"

"She was in bed when she was found. She was naked, the man was wearing a robe, nothing else. The doctor is reasonably certain that intercourse had taken place fairly recently. Semen stains on her legs and on the bedding. We'll know more later of course." The Commissioner looked at the shocked face in front of him.

" Does Michael . . . does Mr. Ainsley know any of this?"

" Yes sir. I've just left him."

" Where is he?"

" At his office."

" I'd better go. Do you need me here Mr. Adams?"

" I expect the officer in charge will want to talk to you sir but that can be arranged later."

" Yes of course, any time Commissioner." Fox paused at the door and looked back at the policeman. " I have the feeling that apart from having a new Home Secretary, soon you will be having quite a lot of new faces in government and new policies to go with them." He shook his head slowly and walked out. A moment later the Commissioner heard the street door close and he walked through to the Home Secretary's study. The officer in charge was the Superintendent who had been responsible for the investigation into Evans. He came over to the Commissioner.

" Good morning sir. Nasty business. Don't think there is much doubt. He's taken cyanide. You don't drink that stuff by mistake and you don't let anyone else do it to you either. And there's a note. Usual thing. To his wife and Linda, the daughter. Saying he's sorry and he loves them both. There's the note on the desk." Adams walked over and read the note without touching the paper. The wording was odd but to the Commissioner like the Superintendent, it was immediately understandable.

" Poor man," he murmured, unknowingly expressing the same thought as the Prime Minister had done earlier. He nodded and went out into the hall. The Superintendent followed him.

" I heard something about the Foreign Secretary's wife. Is it true? Was she dead in bed with some fancy man?" Adams looked at him bleakly for a moment and thought of remonstrating. Then he nodded slowly.

" Something like that," he said.

190

"Christ what a night. What a week in fact."

"Yes, what a week." The Commissioner let himself out of the front door and walked to his car. He gave the driver his instructions and leaned back on the cushioned seat and closed his eyes.

*　　*　　*

The meeting between Comoy and Hunt at the Embassy started at eight o'clock on Wednesday morning. It was not going well. It was Comoy's fault and he knew it.

"Look Lewis, give me something, anything that I can hang what you're saying on to. It's no damned good you having these, these flights of fancy if we can't find some truth, some fact that makes them all make sense."

"There aren't any facts Frank. It's just a feeling."

"A feeling isn't good enough Lewis. You've had the feeling all along, since Harry Walters turned up that fingerprint. But nothing that has happened since fits in. It can't have been the man from Dallas who did all this."

"Wait a minute. Let's start at the beginning. One, we have the fact that a man who was in Dallas fifteen years ago is here in England."

"Was here, over a week ago, we don't know he is still here."

"Alright, was here. Fact two, the only person to get a good look at him, the girl, was murdered. Fact three, there have been two attempts on the life of the President."

"It's too big a leap Lewis. You can't tie that into the first two facts and you can't even tie those two together, not as a fact. No, I'm sorry Lewis, we can't jump to those kind of conclusions."

"What is the alternative?"

"Right. Fact. The gun that fired the six shots on Tuesday morning was in the glove box of that Jaguar. Fact. In the

191

same glove box was a shirt and hat matching the description of those worn by the gunman. Fact. The man in the Jaguar had money on him. For him a lot of money. Fact. He is a known criminal. Fact. There was . . ."

" Stop a minute Frank. He was a local tough. Not a professional assassin. And you don't kill Presidents for five hundred pounds."

" Then what was he doing with the gun?"

" He was set up."

" Set up for what?"

" He's the Oswald."

" The . . .?"

" He's the one we all turn our attention to. Only this time he goes off with a bang instead of being shot by an onlooker."

" Oh, wait a minute, you're not saying Jack Ruby was put in by our man with the fingerprint."

" Maybe not. Maybe he had something else planned for Oswald and Ruby did it before he got there. I don't know. What matters is that the system is the same. We are all doing exactly what the Dallas police did. We are jumping to conclusions. We have more evidence than we know what to do with and we're making the same kind of mess they made. And we thought they were amateurs. We haven't learned much."

" Okay Lewis, I'm not going to talk you out of it. What do you want to do?"

" We assume our man was behind it and he's either going to try again or he's had enough and is getting out."

" Wait a minute you're not making sense. If he set up the Chinaman then he must be ready to get out. But the President isn't dead. So if he tries again he'll give away the fact that the Chinaman was a set-up."

" Yes."

" So you want it both ways?"

" Yes."

" Okay Lewis you're the boss."

" For the moment."

" What's that supposed to mean?"

" Retirement is suddenly an attractive thought."

" Not you. You're not the type."

" Maybe not but the President seems to think so."

" Okay what do we do?"

" We keep a maximum surveillance on the President. We assume there will be another attempt. We also assume our man is getting out. A full watch on all ports and air terminals."

" That's for the police, we can't do that."

" Adams will co-operate. Get at least one of our men into each of his teams at all main exit points. We also follow up your theory and keep close to the inquiry into Ronald Kwok."

" Right. I'll put Draycott onto following up the investigation. I'll get onto Adams and organise the port watch. Will you take care of the President's guard?"

" Okay Frank, bear with me. There is more here than we can see on the surface. And we still haven't touched on the biggest mystery of all."

" What's that?"

" How he missed. Whether it was the man from Dallas or your Mr. Kwok, how the hell did he miss blowing the President's head off from that range?"

*   *   *

Raymond Adams was still tired and the growing mountain of information and evidence, some contradictory and some unrelated grew steadily. Only one minor spark of brightness had appeared in the gloom. The Bomb Squad had received a tip-off and on following it up they had arrested three men and a woman all members of a known group of declared anarchists. With them the Squad had found enough evidence to link them with the bomb-van that had crashed into the car in Upper Brook Street. One of the men had made a statement admitting, claiming was a better word for it, responsibility. But their target had been Charles Fox not the President. Adams was inclined to believe it. He had passed the information on to the Americans and had wearily pressed on with other matters.

He had closed the case on the Home Secretary. The file on his suicide would remain open until the Coroner had given his verdict. Then that too would be closed. A sad business was his final thought but at least it was all neatly put together. Not like the other problems that showed no signs of solving themselves and which were proving unbreakable despite the number of men involved in the enquiries. The search for the gunman who had penetrated the shield around the President with astonishing ease went on and privately Adams was sure nothing would come of it. He was far from convinced that Comoy's theories were close to the truth. Even so Ronald Kwok did not fit the mould he would have made for a man hired to attempt an assassination of a Head of State. And the Bomb Squad's report on the explosion in Kwok's car was slightly unsettling. An inertia switch to fire the detonator suggested either gross carelessness on the part of the man handling the explosive or that someone else had set it up. But no one else had been seen near the car. And the driver could not have driven there with the switch set. He rubbed his eyes wearily as the telephone rang. It was the American Colonel, Hunt.

" Yes Colonel, what can I do for you?"

" Can you brief me on port and airport watches?"

" Extensive Colonel, as extensive as we can make them. We have covered everywhere we can think of as a likely point of departure, legal and illegal. The main problem is of course

194

the fact that we are in the middle of the tourist season. We have people arriving and departing in their tens of thousands. Particularly at Heathrow and Gatwick."

" Perhaps we can help. We can send a few men out to assist. They all have descriptions of the man, we, well, the man Lewis thinks is behind all this. Based on Harry Walters' description of course."

" Glad to have any help you can give. I take it you incline towards the theory that Kwok is our man."

" Between ourselves Commissioner I do. Whether he was in it on his own or not I don't know. Perhaps our man was the planner in which case he is trying to get out. I cannot believe there will be another attempt."

"I hope you're right. I think you are but until your President and all the other Heads of State are back in their own countries I shall assume the worst."

" So shall we all Commissioner. Look I'll get some men out to Heathrow and to Gatwick right away. I'll go with one of the groups myself and get things organised. Who is in charge there?" The Commissioner gave the American the information he wanted and went back to brooding over the problems he faced.

*　　*　　*

The deaths of Janet Ainsley and the security man Perring were his next headache. It seemed on the surface to be cut and dried. An attractive woman and a younger good-looking man. A husband too busy to give his full attention. A routine triangle. Except there was no suicide note. And the man had had an extra unlisted telephone. He had already put C.11 onto the trail of Perring and he knew someone would be checking slowly through his records. Perhaps something would turn up, perhaps not. In any event that would be an investigation that would take its course. At least the be-

195

trayed husband had not done it. There was one thing about having a Foreign Secretary for a suspect. His movements were easily checked.

*　　*　　*

He thought for a moment about the meeting with the Prime Minister, at the Home Secretary's house. Charles Fox had been right. There would soon be a new government. The suicide of the Home Secretary would be put down to overwork, strain, all known hazards of the duties men in high places faced daily. In fact it was surprising more did not break down. But in the backs of the minds of the electorate would be planted a small seed of doubt and that seed would be watered by the inevitable scandal of the manner and the circumstances of the death of Janet Ainsley. Soon he would have a new man over him, with new ideas and new policies and new prejudices and new peccadilloes. Adams sighed and drew a file towards him. He began to work and in a few minutes his concentration blotted out the problems of the future, the problems of the present were enough.

*　　*　　*

Frank Hunt managed to break away twelve men without reducing the Presidential and investigative groups to a dangerously low level. He sent seven of the twelve to Heathrow under the command of an able senior agent and he went with the smaller group to Gatwick. At the last moment he had acquired an extra man in the shape of a pale but determined Harry Walters.

"Are you sure you're up to it Inspector?" he had asked.

"Yes, quite sure sir. The doctor reckoned a few days sitting doing nothing but that's the way doctors usually talk. They think they are the only ones with jobs that make them

196

indispensable."

" How bad was it?"

" Not too bad at all really. High up on the shoulder, flesh wound only. No serious loss of blood, that was because it happened right where I could get immediate treatment."

" Okay. No doubt we can use you."

" Where are you heading?"

" Gatwick. We're keeping a watch for your friend."

" Good. I hope we find him there." There was a hard note in the Inspector's voice that the colonel did not miss.

* * *

The officer in charge of the impossible task of watching for a man with the vaguest of descriptions was grateful for the help and particularly so when the colonel offered to stay on himself for an hour or two. The Colonel's men and Harry Walters were deployed around the airport with an organised watch at each of the gates as flights were called. The Colonel walked over to the gate that would be handling the noon flight to Faro at about twenty minutes to twelve. He found Harry Walters already there. The policeman looked pale and very ill.

" Inspector, you don't look so good. Go and find some-where to sit down for a while."

" Thank you sir. I do feel rotten. I think I'll stay here though. The nearest seats are over there," he waved his good arm, " I might not make it that far." The Colonel looked at him for a moment and then nodded briefly before turning away.

* * *

Stellman had parked the white Cortina in one of the car parks close to the airport and had been transported to the terminal by mini-coach. He had timed things well. He would have no more than the irritating hour that officialdom decreed had to be spent idly waiting before a flight. He checked in his suitcase and waited patiently with the other two hundred tourists who were taking the same flight to Portugal. When the flight was called he joined the file of people approaching the desk where passports were checked. He saw the tall military-looking figure standing near to the official who scrutinised the passports.

*　　*　　*

Hunt searched the faces of the passengers approaching the desk. Then he let his eyes range over beyond them and he looked in turn at each of the faces of the people standing watching as they always did at airports. His eyes suddenly focused on one of those faces. He turned to Walters who was half-standing, half-leaning against a counter.

" Inspector, how do you feel?"

" A little better sir."

" Up to doing something?"

" Yes sir. What's wrong?"

" Probably nothing but look over there. The tall thin man in the blue suit, next to the woman in the big white hat. Got him?"

" Yes."

" His name's LeReuesz. French intelligence. Probably coincidence but it might be an idea to follow him."

" Yes sir." Walters walked away from the desk his eyes fixed on the man the American had pointed out. He passed within a few feet of Stellman who was still in the queue approaching the desk.

*　　*　　*

When it was Stellman's turn he handed over Carter's passport with no trace of expression on his face. The official glanced at Carter's photograph and up at Stellman. The fluorescent light in the notice board over their heads reflected on the lenses of the rimless glasses worn by the military looking man and made his eyes expressionless pools of light.

The official handed back the passport and Stellman walked on and followed those already through the barrier down the walkway towards the aircraft.

* * *

Fifteen minutes later, only two minutes behind schedule, the aircraft took off. Colonel Hunt wandered away towards another boarding area. After that flight had left he went in search of the police officer in charge and announced that he had to return to London. Just before he left Gatwick he stepped into a kiosk and made a long distance telephone call.

* * *

Stellman dozed easily throughout the flight to Faro and was relaxed and refreshed when the aircraft landed. He took a taxi from the airport into the town and on the way he wrote a short message to Carter giving him the locations of the hire cars that had to be returned. At the bottom of the page he added a note advising Carter to empty the boot of the white Cortina. The motor-cycle would be a bonus for him. He slipped the note into Carter's passport and sealed it into an envelope ready to hand to the barman at the Hotel Eva. An hour and a half later Stellman was in an Iberian Airways DC-7 flying east over the Mediterranean. He whistled softly to himself for most of the flight. He was happy. He was going home.

*   *   *

The old man was sitting at the window when the two younger men came into the room. For a moment he did not turn, his eyes fixed on the moon in the dark September sky. Then he turned and looked at them. The creases re-arranged themselves on his face. The younger of the two men knew what that meant. The old man was smiling.

" Well?"

" Better than we expected."

" Tell me."

" Polls first. We know they can be unreliable but the last one before Leeson went to London showed he was the most unpopular President there has been since Polls were conducted. He was set to lose in November by a colossal margin."

" And now?"

" A complete reversal. He will equal Truman's defeat of Dewey, at least."

" Good, good. What else?"

" Congress will approve the new arms programme. And there will be a resumption of underground tests in the spring."

" Then detente between America and China is finished?"

" Dead."

" Dead is for a long time."

" Dead enough to see us all in our graves."

" And that is long enough?"

" I . . ." the young man broke off not sure if the old man was joking with him. A rustling papery sound escaped from the old man's throat. It was a laugh. The young man laughed too and after a moment the thin man in glasses joined in.

*   *   *

After a moment the old man closed his eyes and the others fell silent. He spoke again without opening them.

" No one has spoken directly to Leeson?"

" No."

" Good."

" Will you tell him?"

" I doubt it. He might not see our point of view."

" He should be grateful."

" He should be but he is a small man. He will think only of his pain and discomfort. And his fear."

" The security forces do not believe the Chinese were responsible."

" Of course they don't. We never expected they would but it is not important. What is important is what the press and television have made the people think. And they think it was a Chinese plot. A plot that failed. Governments in the end do what they think the people will favour."

" What about Comoy?"

" A clever man. He is being retired." The old man paused for a moment. " You tidied up Perring's Australian connection?"

" Yes. We thought about laying a link to the Chinese there too, giving a tie-in to the other business but we decided it would be too dangerous. Perring's trail was too easily followed after Australia."

" So what about Australia?"

" It was dealt with immediately we received Stellman's letter."

" Good."

" What happened to Stellman," the thin man spoke for the first time. " I know he got out but how did he do it?"

" Exactly as planned. Hunt saw him leave."

" Colonel Hunt?" The old man laughed again at the note of incredulity in the thin man's voice.

" Yes. One of my secrets."

" Then he set up the route for Stellman?"

" Yes, but the Sleeper arranged for the car to follow the right route on the right day."

" How?"

" I don't know. He had some hold on the Home Secretary, and he in turn gave orders to the route selector."

" What did the Sleeper have on Evans?"

" I don't know but whatever it was it was strong. Strong enough to make the man poison himself when he found what he was involved in."

" What about the Sleeper? He'll be weaker now."

" No matter. He will come again. There's time." The old man closed his eyes again. Silence fell again. The young man gathered his papers together and put them into his briefcase. He stood up and looked down at the old man.

" That fingerprint. It was as well we did not know it was Stellman's. What is being done about it?"

" As you say it was as well we did not know. If we had we might have sent someone else, someone who is not as accurate with a gun as he is. Even then it wouldn't have mattered if it hadn't been for that interfering English policeman." The old man's voice suddenly took on a vicious tone that surprised the thin man. " He should have paid for his interference. Stellman's bullet should have been fatal." The young man merely nodded and quietly asked his question again.

" What are we doing about Stellman's fingerprints?" The old man ignored him and was still thinking about other things.

" The French had to interfere as well. Damn good job Hunt spotted the man at the airport. Might have been co-incidence but my guess is they were onto Stellman. Damned if I know how." There was a long silence and the young man watched the old man from under hooded eyelids. He said nothing. Privately he felt a quickening of his pulse. The old man had never before shown the signs of weakening pettiness. It could be the first signs of the thing he had waited for for so long. If it was it had come at a good moment. With Leeson re-elected to the White House and with an increased majority there would be great days ahead. More power. Greater wealth. And he wanted both, unlike the old man who only wanted power. He already had great wealth. He came out of his reverie and realised there was only silence in the room. He looked at the old man again. He appeared to be asleep. He reached forward and touched the back of the liver-spotted hand. The old man opened his eyes.

" What are we going to do about Stellman's fingerprint?"

" Nothing. We might not have to use him again. If we do then we can use the fact of the fingerprint to ensure that we do not have to pay as much. It is about time we had a hold on him. And it will compensate us for his carelessness."

" Carelessness?"

" He should never have left a print at Dallas. Then there would have been no need to have killed the girl. Not that she matters. And he should have spotted the Frenchman on his tail. That all shows carelessness."

" We got what we wanted. No one else could have been relied upon to have done that."

" Maybe not." The young man stood up. " Anything more?" The old man shook his head and the young man walked to the door. He waited there for the thin man and held the door open to permit him to pass through into the corridor. The young man stayed in the opening for a moment watching the old man thoughtfully. Then he closed the door gently.

" When do we meet again?" the thin man asked.

" At the end of November will be soon enough. After Leeson has been re-elected. There will be a lot to do. We have to assist in drafting the first of the bills he will be bringing before Congress. The increase in defence spending.

And the boost for space research. Our companies there are having a very lean time. And we have to accelerate the turn away from the social reforms. We cannot afford them, we need unemployment to really bite." The thin man nodded. He was silent for a moment. Then he nodded again, this time as a gesture towards the door.

"He seems tired."

"He is old."

"Yes." The two men looked at one another. Then the young man turned and walked away down the corridor. After a moment the other man followed him.

*   *   *

In the room the old man pressed the button on the arm of his wheel chair and glided across the floor to the window. He stayed there watching the tail-lights of the two cars as they drove away towards the glow that hung in the sky over Houston. He watched until the red lights had disappeared and then he reached forward and pressed the wall switch and the electric motor hummed as the curtains slid across the window. He stayed where he was for a long time thinking. He had not missed the last enquiring look the young man had given him.

He knew what that meant. And he knew what to do about it. In the old days he would have simply fought any opposition with whatever was at his disposal. Even his fists if that had seemed the best way. Now he had everything he needed to fight or remove opposition. But he missed the physical pleasure of the beatings he had administered in the old days. He closed his eyes and dreamed of them. He remembered them vividly. More than he remembered his wives who were little more than shadows on an otherwise clear landscape. He thought again about the young man. He wanted to give him a chance because he knew he was the best man to take over. But only when he was ready to go and that was not to be for a long time to come. That meant the young man had to go. A pity. But it was unavoidable.

*   *   *

Several thousand miles away the Sleeper worked at his desk. Since the abortive end of the conference he had gradually added things together, things that answered a lot of questions and explained a lot of mysteries. The final message from his Texan masters had cleared up all outstanding doubts. The message had been less laconic than usual: Congratulations, all went as planned, wait.

He was pleased that everything had worked well. It had enabled him to understand more fully the part he had played and also it brought to his mind, for the first time, the full reality of what he was doing. His was a permanent role. Everything he did was for them. Nothing he did was for the country he nominally served. He had only one master. He also knew what was meant this time when the message ended with the one word " wait." He was there for the rest of his life. He might visit his homeland but he would never return. America was no longer his country. He would remain an Englishman until the day he died.

*   *   *

It had been a long time. A very long time since that day over thirty years before when he had stepped into the shoes of a dead soldier on the battlefield outside Berlin. A soldier who had no relatives and few friends and who bore a likeness sufficient to enable him to pass into his new life. A life that had given him a great deal. Position and authority, not a lot of tangible fruition, no great wealth, but position and authority which were more important to him. He smiled to himself. His masters had picked him well, they knew him.

They knew that what he did he did for the love of his country, love fashioned in their image perhaps but love none the less for that. He had a wife for whom he felt affection and he usually enjoyed what he did. Not always but often enough to provide the compensation he needed for all the things he did not have.

*   *   *

He sighed deeply and looked at the pile of papers on his desk. There was a lot to do, there was always a lot to do. When the winter was over there would be an election. That would mean more work. Work that would be made less palatable than usual because this time there was little doubt that the election would be lost. A pity that but it was not the end of the road. Merely a set-back. He would not be out of office for ever. People's memories were short and when the time was right he would come back to power, he had no doubt about that at all.

*   *   *

He picked up his pen and began making marginal notes on the first of the piles of papers that needed his attention. He paused and lit a cigarette and as he did so he glanced out of the window into the garden. It was the same view he saw from one floor above in his bedroom. It always relaxed him, a garden of tranquillity in the heart of London, so surprising to find peace there at the hub of his political world. He smiled to himself, he even thought like an Englishman these days. He bent his head to the work and was soon lost in the problems of his alien home. He would lose the Spring election but until then Charles Fox was still Prime Minister.

*   *   *